THE HIGH STEAKS
MURDER

AN ARIZONA SUMMERS MYSTERY
BOOK TWO

SUSAN KEENE

Publishing Coordinator – Sharon Kizziah-Holmes
Cover Design – Jaycee DeLorenzo

Published by Bent Willow Books

ISBN -13: 978-1-951772-39-0

DEDICATION

To Sue Sears and her infinite patience.

ACKNOWLEDGMENTS

To the best group of friends a person could have. A special thanks to Sharon-Kizziah-Holmes, of Paperback Press, for her formatting expertise, and Jaycee DeLorenzo of Sweet 'n Spicy Designs, for her covers.

Author's Note: Please enjoy the first chapter of Wedding Cake Murder on page 228 of this book.

CHAPTER ONE

The ringing of my cell phone woke me at 2:35. Nutmeg jumped out of bed on the first ring and stood between me and the open bedroom door. She always ran to the same spot between me and the rest of the apartment in case something unexpected happened.

I could only guess it was how she prepared to protect me if someone came in the front door. Since I lived in a second-floor apartment I had only one door.

My caller ID read Liz Austin. I shook the cobwebs from my mind and answered it. "Liz, are you okay?" She sounded out of breath and her normally low voice resounded in the high pitch range. "Arizona, I'm downstairs at your front door. Let me in."

I looked down at my clothes. My sleep shorts were as long as capris and my tee shirt looked respectable. I ran down to unlock the door without putting on a robe. Nutmeg beat me down the stairs, stood and wagged her tail at Liz through the glass.

"Arizona, thank goodness. I didn't know where else to go."

I looked at her clothes and turned away from her as the coppery smell of blood assaulted my nose. "Blood?" I stated the obvious.

She wore a pair of grey yoga pants and an oversized tee shirt with a picture of the Golden Girls on the front, and blood, lots of blood. Her disheveled blond hair hung around her face. It looked as though she used vampire shampoo. She self-consciously ran her hands through it and they came away sticky and with her hair caught on them.

"Liz, what happened? Did you have an accident?"

"Is it okay if I come in?"

I took her arm and gently helped her inside. "Geez Liz, I'm sorry."

She brought her bloody hands to her face to cover her eyes as she began to sob. "It's Mick."

"Mick Dudley," I asked, "your ex?"

She lowered her hands to answer me. The blood on her cheeks gave her the look of a painted porcelain doll. "He's dead."

I motioned for her to go ahead of me up the stairs to my apartment. Nutmeg stayed by her side and let out a small whine with her every step.

"Is that Mick's blood? Tell me you didn't have anything to do with his death."

She looked down at her clothes. "It was horrible. I heard someone moan. It was obvious whoever made the noise needed help. It was Mick and he died in my arms."

I motioned to the couch. "Here, sit and tell me exactly what happened." I put my hand on her arm. "Wait a minute. Let me put a towel down first." I looked down at the dog. "Nutmeg, will you go to the bathroom and bring back a towel."

She barked once and padded off to the bathroom.

While we waited for Nutmeg to return, I studied Liz. She was a slight woman. In grade school she had the title of the smallest girl in our class. At this moment, she looked as though she'd better sit, before she fell.

My trusty dog dragged a bath towel from the other room and I draped it over the couch like a seat cover and motioned for her to sit.

I'd known Liz Austin since; well, forever. One of her finest traits was her ability to keep her cool even if the world fell apart around her. This night she'd lost her composure.

I nodded. I doubt she saw me. I'm not a doctor but with my limited expertise I knew she was in shock. Her eyes were focused somewhere over my head. Her pupils resembled needle points. She took deep halting breaths as children do when they've cried for an extended period of time. "Tonight, I had yoga."

She never looked at me. I wondered if she wanted to try to put the events of the night in order and straight in her mind. I tried to plod her along. "So, you had yoga, did you do anything after your class?"

"Yes, a couple of friends and I decided to drive

over to the north side to listen to the band at Charlie's."

I stopped her to ask. "What two ladies went with you?"

"Do you think it's important?" She asked.

"I assume Mick was murdered. Why else would you come to my home in the middle of the night? Do you believe one of them had anything to do with his death? "

"No, they were with me until they dropped me off on Cobblestone near my apartment. They would have to fly to make it around the building to kill Mick before I walked around the corner to my apartment. It's only two doors away.

"Martha Beatty, the new clerk at Aunt Tillie's Treasures and Dee Hampton. I'm sure you know Dee. She opened the Gray Goose Herb Shoppe a couple of years ago. Neither of them lived in Moonstone Lake when Mick did."

When I didn't say anything, she continued. She tucked both legs under her so they were on the towel and not on the upholstery. She trudged on with her story. "A couple of times during the evening I thought I saw Mick. He sat alone at the opposite end of the bar from where we sat. I looked at him out of the corner of my eye more than once, but he paid no attention to me.

"He wore old jeans, a pale-yellow polo not tucked in and a baseball cap pulled down so far it nearly covered his entire face. He was noticeably thinner than the last time I saw him. But it was him. You can't be married to a man and not recognize the way he moves and his mannerisms.

"I didn't notice until Dee and Martha pulled away. Without their headlights I realized the street lights were out as was the motion light above my apartment door."

Liz began to talk so fast I couldn't follow her. "Liz, slow down. Take a few deep breaths

before you begin again. At this point I see no need to hurry."

She did as I said. "I didn't think too much of it, she said, until I heard a noise. The hair stood up on the back of my neck. Ary, my heart never beat so hard in my life. It didn't sound like it came from a human, more like an animal in distress.

"I had my pen light in my hand so I could see to unlock my door. I started up the stairs and I heard someone weakly call my name. I knew it was Mick. My first instinct was to run up the stairs and deadbolt myself inside my apartment. When I took a step closer to him, he had on the same clothes I saw at Charlie's. It was Mick, for sure." She stopped on her own this time. "May I have a drink of water?"

I went to the kitchen and came back with two glasses of water. While I was in the other room Nutmeg jumped on the couch and sat next to her. Liz put her hand on the dog, and absently petted her back. I hoped she didn't transfer any blood to Nutmeg but the blood looked dry.

I wondered if the blood itched. Now it was dry and the coppery smell had faded, it looked more and more like finger paint. I thought it best not to voice my observation.

Liz took a long drink and set the glass on the end table. "I was terrified. You know some of our relationship when we were married. I've often wondered, over the years, why he changed so abruptly. He went from silly, funny, loving guy, to a man I didn't know. He became suspicious of everyone. He wouldn't smile or go out. I tried to talk to him but he didn't let me in on whatever went wrong in his life."

I moved to the couch and sat on the other side of her. Her voice quivered, hands shook, and now instead of staring into space, she glanced from side to side, to the window, and then the door. She looked terrified.

"Something pulled me in his direction. Oh my, Ary, he was covered in blood. He lay on his side toward me. His pupils were huge. I knew he was dying. I rolled him over onto his back.

"A knife stuck out of his chest. I pulled it out and threw it down. When I did, blood gushed out. I tried to give him CPR. The harder I tried the more he bled."

"Liz, if the blood came out fast, he was alive. His heart pushed it out with every beat. He had to be alive."

Liz looked at me as though I were an alien. "I sat next to him; mesmerized. I couldn't force myself to move or look around. I didn't think to call anyone. He startled me with a halting breath and whispered to me. I put my ear next to his mouth. His words were clear. I didn't mistake them. It's the last words he uttered. He said, *the money was mine. They were supposed to love me and take care of me. They threw me to the curb for money.*

I put a hand on her shoulder. "I don't want to

make you feel worse than you do, but you should have dialed 911, or at least called Keith on his cell phone."

Keith Wesley was the new chief of police, and Liz Austin, a star reporter at The Daily Reflection; Moonstone Lake's Newspaper. They worked together on cases and he often singled her out when he needed a certain spin on a story.

"It never entered my mind to call him. After Mick whispered to me; he stopped bleeding. His eyes were cloudy and fixed. I waited for him to take one more breath. It didn't happen.

"I sat next to his lifeless body until the battery went out on my pin light then I panicked. It occurred to me the street lights were out for a reason. A dead body lay in the shadows within five feet of my front door. And not just any body, my ex-husband."

CHAPTER TWO

Liz stood and stretched. "Fear pushed good sense right out the window. You know how dark it is on the side streets off the Boardwalk when the lights are out. I thought I heard noises and saw shadows of figures in every direction I looked. I ran."

She began to shiver. "Go into the bathroom," I said, "and take off those bloody clothes. I'll get a bag to put them in. Keith will want to see them and run tests. I'll find you an outfit to put on."

"Oh, Arizona, I didn't think about it until this minute. Because I fled the scene and didn't call them, the police will think I killed him."

I had nothing to say. I had no idea what I would have done in the same situation. I wasn't afraid of the dark, yet before I had Nutmeg, I slept with a night light. I told myself I didn't want to fall in the night.

Actually, I didn't want anyone I couldn't see to come in and surprise me.

Liz headed for the bathroom and I went in the other direction. I found the smallest clothes I could. Even the clothes I could no longer wear because they were tight would swim on Liz's tiny body. With a tee shirt and sweat pants in my right hand and my phone in my left I opened the bathroom door a crack and handed her the clothes.

She closed the door and I called Keith Wesley. I didn't say much. It wasn't my story to tell. I told him Liz had some trouble earlier in the evening and needed to talk to him. And no, it couldn't wait until morning.

Keith arrived in minutes. Randy Malone, Keith's next in command, knocked on the downstairs door a little later. I ran down and let him in. I didn't have to let Keith in, he had the outside door codes in case of emergency. I hoped Liz didn't notice he let himself in. It wasn't as it seemed.

One of our past employees was responsible for the death of a visitor to Moonstone Lake. He lived in the apartment Liz occupied now. I gave Keith the codes in case he needed to enter in a hurry.

Keith knocked on the door and before he ever stepped inside, he asked, "what's going on here ladies?"

Liz came out of the bathroom, her face freshly scrubbed and wearing my clothes. She rolled the pant legs up on the light blue Capris and pushed them passed her knees so she wouldn't trip and she'd tied the black and red Grateful Dead tee shirt in a knot at the waist. Her long blond hair hung down her back and cascaded around her face. She looked so young and innocent.

I removed the now stained towel from the couch and Liz sat down. Nutmeg claimed the spot next to her and laid her head on Liz's lap.

Keith looked back and forth from Liz to me. "Come on ladies, it's the middle of the night. I know you didn't get us over here to have a beer so let's have it."

Liz began to cry but this time she didn't sob. The tears filled her eyes and ran down her cheeks as she talked. "Mick Dudley is dead. I found him outside of my apartment."

Keith looked at me with a blank stare. "I don't think I've ever heard of Mick Dudley. Someone enlighten me." He said it with an exasperated sigh.

Nutmeg growled at him. He looked from Liz to me to the dog and then said. "Nutmeg, I thought you and I were buddies. What's with the attitude?"

She jumped down from the couch and stood directly in front of him.

"You know how she is. Sit back and relax. She senses your tension and she doesn't like it. Look at the back of her neck. She's in guard mode. Can you take a deep breath, lean back and not look like you may pounce any minute?"

He looked at Nutmeg for a long moment and said. "I'm sorry girl. I'll be nicer."

Nutmeg gave him a paw to shake and went back to her seat next to Liz.

Liz, Randy and I watched the exchange. No one could help but smile. The tension level dropped considerably in the room.

Liz spoke up. "I'm sorry Keith; Mick was my ex-husband. We were married for five years. "We were married when the authorities went to his job and took him out in handcuffs. It was hush-hush. None of us knew exactly what he did or if he did anything. The only people who were allowed to go in and out of the courtroom were Chief Chase, two local lawyers, four men in dark suits and the judge. They didn't allow spectators or the media. I thought they would let me in because I was his wife, but I was wrong. And I was denied access even though I was a reporter for the Moonstone Lake Reflection.

"The entire proceeding took six days. They took Mick away in handcuffs and I didn't hear from him or see him until tonight.

"I heard through the grapevine he was to serve a five-year sentence in the Ozarks Correctional Prison in Leslie. I never did get a straight answer as to why. Chief Chase told me the files were sealed and he didn't know himself what happened for sure. Mick obviously had a side to him he didn't reveal to me. Of course, I was devastated and divorced him.

"About nine months ago I received a letter from the warden at Ozark Correctional. He said Mick was to be released in three months. One of the conditions of his parole was not to get within one hundred yards of me. He wasn't to call, write or come to my place of employment.

"Since he's been free, I haven't heard a word until tonight when I saw him at Charlie's and again when I found him fatally wounded near my apartment door. Why would they make a stipulation like that when he walked out on a five-year marriage without a word to me?"

Keith glanced at his watch. "How long ago did all of this take place? It's almost three a.m."

Liz looked down to avoid meeting Keith's gaze. "It was after midnight, maybe twelve-thirty."

Keith took on a professional air and an accusatory tone. "Seems late to be out on a work night, do you do that often?"

I laid my hand on top of hers and squeezed. "No," she said, "I went out with the girls from my Yoga class. We went to Charlie's to listen to the band. One of the women's brothers is the drummer. Funny thing is I thought I saw Mick there. I knew he wouldn't be stupid enough to come near me and chance another jail term. With the ball cap pulled down over his face and the weight he'd lost; I'm most likely the only one in the bar who recognized him.

Keith took his phone out of this pocket and made a call. "Jess, can you get your crew together and meet me behind the Hoof and Mane Beauty Shop on the Boardwalk. I think there has been a murder near the apartment in the back."

For the first time since he arrived, the Chief smiled at Liz. "We'll get to the bottom of this. It is unusual for an adult to have a closed trial. It is a tool most usually used for children when they make a mistake so it won't follow them all their lives. If they stay out of trouble and become model citizens, the records are expunged.

"It doesn't mean adult files are never sealed. I will scour the files when I get to the office and see what I can find out. I can also call Chief Chase and see what he knows." He knelt in front of Liz. "I'm going to leave now. I want you to go into the kitchen with Randy and write down everything you remember about yesterday and tonight. Don't leave anything out.

"Depending on what I find out at the crime scene, I'll either see you tonight at the station or tomorrow."

Before Keith had a chance to leave, his phone rang. He listened carefully, and said, "are you sure?" He didn't take his eyes off of Liz. "Okay, thanks, I'll bring her with me."

He looked at me, Liz and then Randy. "There is no body anywhere around your apartment. I'm going to have to ask you to come with me. I need to know exactly where he was and what you saw and heard."

While Keith talked to her, I went into the bathroom to retrieve her shoes. They were brown leather sandals with straps that crisscrossed in the front and a tiny strap across the heel. They were caked with blood.

Trancelike, Liz slipped the shoes on and stood. Randy gently took her arm by the elbow and escorted her toward the front door.

Keith stopped them with a question. "Are you sure the man was dead?"

She shook her head. "He wasn't breathing. I tried to give him CPR but it caused blood to ooze from his chest. He made a noise and when I leaned down he said something. It was faint

but his words were clear. He said, *the money was mine. They were supposed to love me and take care of me. They threw me to the curb for money.*

Keith let out a loud breath. "Didn't it dawn on

13

you to call an ambulance and the police?"

Her soft voice now held a hard edge. "Keith. He was dead. I know dead when I see it."

"Are you ready to go?"

She shook her head yes.

"Are you going to the crime scene? I asked.

He looked back at me. "Yes, to the crime scene."

Nutmeg stood, stretched on the couch and jumped down. "Can Nutmeg and I come along?"

He stopped and put his hands on his hips. "Arizona, you are not the police. I don't think it is appropriate."

Liz spoke up. "It would help me if she were there."

I said nothing. Nutmeg stood close to me. The look Keith gave me was anything but friendly.

One of the truths I learned over the years was the first person who speaks in a standoff, loses. I could out wait him.

He looked down and said. "Okay, but don't touch anything. Randy, you take Liz. Don't let her out of the car until I get there."

CHAPTER THREE

At the crime scene Jess Morgan, the lead CSI officer, a tall slim fellow who had the body of a runner, shouted to Keith as we got out of the car. "Hey Chief, glad you're here. Like I said, we can't find a body. We've looked two blocks in each direction. We did find a bloody knife. Most likely it's the murder weapon considering the amount of blood on it."

Keith walked closer. I stayed back since I didn't want to get in the way.

Crime tape started on the Boardwalk and cordoned off the entrance to the alley. It ran from the side of the Hoof and Mane and ended at the beginning of Cobblestone Lane at the other end of the alley. The beauty shop had the only upstairs apartment. The backs of the rest of the buildings were storage space for the store in front of it. Cute European style outdoor tables with green and white paneled umbrellas and wrought iron chairs painted in the same color scheme lined the sidewalks on both sides of the Boardwalk. One of the patrol officers had looped the starting end of the bright yellow tape around the leg of the table closest to the alley.

Now instead of a lovely retreat, the area looked as if a herd of cattle had run through it with a posse of cowboys behind them. The Moonstone Police, Highway Patrol, Sheriff's vehicles and an ambulance were double parked all the way down Cobblestone Lane with their lights flashing.

The shops on Cobblestone were mostly what I referred to as *secondary* shops. From east to west sat Eagle Groceries, Miller's Drug Store, The Ginger Cow, a takeout only Chinese restaurant, a Kettle Corn Stand, Goodwill and The Junk Room.

"Did you find blood or any other evidence?" Keith asked Jess.

Randy walked Liz closer to the scene. Keith called back over his shoulder. "You guys wait there."

"Yeah chief," Jess answered pointing with a mag light in the direction of the Boardwalk. There's a lot of blood here and we bagged a wallet. Identity on the cards inside is Mitchell James Dudley, age 33, 6'2" and 220 pounds. The street address listed says Indianapolis, Indiana. He's a big guy to be hauling around, especially if he's dead weight. There are drag marks running out to Cobblestone Lane. They end at the curb."

"So, someone came back for the body. That's

strange unless he had something on him they didn't want us to see. Keith pointed toward the street passed Liz's apartment. "Widen your search. Ask Edwin at Eagle Grocery if he saw or heard anything. He's open all night.".

Keith turned toward us once again and motioned us forward. I knew Keith well enough to know he didn't mean me and Nutmeg. I went up within hearing distance but stayed far enough back no one could fault us for being too close.

Keith put all of his attention on Liz. "Go through it with me. Start from the time you got out of your friend's car"

She and Randy and Keith walked toward Cobblestone Lane. No one could have dropped her off within blocks of her apartment if they stopped near the Boardwalk, driving down it had been prohibited for years.

I saw her hands move up and down as she pointed and motioned. She nodded toward the lights, she said were out, yet now shined brightly to lead their way. I had the sensation I was watching an old silent movie.

The killer or killers disabled the lights and took the body. There had to be a clue on the body or maybe something about the body itself they didn't want found."

I closed my eyes and tried to visualize the Mitchell Dudley I knew. He and Liz came in the restaurant a few times when they were together. He was well over six feet tall in the seventh grade. He never made it to school on time. He told the teacher he was late because he had to shave. No one could deny it was probably true. His hair reminded me of rust, not bright enough to be called red and too dark to be called auburn. When we were about eight years old, I tried to call him Rusty at which time he doubled up this fist and socked me on the shoulder. You couldn't call Mick handsome or pretty but I thought he was cute. His eyes were such a deep brown I could see my own reflection when I talked to him face to face. I don't remember him until third grade. I'd have to ask Mom if she remembered him any younger.

I could tell Liz had been through her story with Keith. I walked closer to see and hear what would happen next.

Keith turned toward Randy, "Would you ask the electric company to check into whether there has been a power outage in this area in the last thirty- six hours? And when you see Jess ask him to dust the light bulb over the apartment door and the one on the side of the building for fingerprints."

The two men talked; Liz walked over to her apartment door. Her purse lay on the ground with its contents on the concrete. She jumped when Keith said from behind her, "Can you tell if anything is missing?"

"Not off hand. It would take me some time. I carry a lot of stuff both for work and personal." She brightened up a little. "Look, there are my keys, in the keyhole."

"Do you remember unlocking the door or do you think someone else did?"

Her smile disappeared as quickly as it came. "I don't have any idea. I'll have to take some time and go over the events again in my mind. It's jumbled now."

"Okay, Liz. Let's go over everything one more time before you lose any of the facts."

My heart broke for her. Anyone could see she was too exhausted to think. At one time she became confused and said the body laid facing the other direction. I wanted to take up for her, but I also didn't want to be banned from tagging along to crime scenes because I butted in.

"My friends let me off in front of my apartment. As you can see, the door is adjacent to the street. I walked to my door and realized the motion light was dark. As I dug through my handbag for the penlight I carry, it dawned on me the street lights on Cobblestone were all out, at least the ones I could see.

"I looked down the alley between the two buildings and I didn't see lights there either. I had my keys in one hand and the little flashlight in the other. I stuck the key in the lock and heard a moan.

"At first I thought it could be an animal but then I heard a distinct voice. It belonged to Mick Dudley."

Keith who stood well over six feet tall, bent his knees and rested his palms on them so he was closer to Liz's face. "You felt safe enough to walk over to the man who walked out on you, you divorced and had not seen in five years?"

Liz's eyes filled with tears, but I knew her well enough to know she would not cry. She might lose her temper if she couldn't get her point across, but not cry.

Keith stayed in his shortened stance and said. "Earlier you stated you had not talked to him or heard from him for over five years, that his voice was nearly inaudible and you couldn't see his face. Is that correct?"

"Yes, but I knew it was him. He sat at the bar in plain view for at least two hours. There are some things you don't forget about a man when you've been married to him."

Keith raised himself to his full height. "So how many times did he call you before you went to him?"

"Just once, I think."

"And even though there were no lights around and it was pitch black; you went to him."

"I had my penlight," she said.

I knew my face burned with anger at the way Keith treated our friend. He looked up and smiled at me. In that instant, I realized he had to be more thorough because she held a special place in our hearts. After two or three deep breaths I relaxed.

"What happened when you went to him? Did he say anything?" Keith asked.

"Yes, as I told you earlier, he said, *the money was mine. They were supposed to love me and take care of me. They threw me to the curb for money.* I told you that before," she said with a bite in her voice.

Keith gave her a strange look and for the first time he looked at me. I thought he was looking for an answer so I said. "She told me what he said earlier, at my place. You were not there yet. She is exhausted."

He looked back to Liz. "Do those words mean anything to you? Did he ever mention having money hiding somewhere or someone taking money he had?"

"No, it doesn't mean anything to me. My head has been spinning since he died in my arms. One thing I'm sure of is if he had any money, he didn't share the news with me."

Keith put his hand lightly on her shoulder. "I'm going into your apartment to look around. You alright with that?"

She shook her head *yes*.

Randy is going to take you to the station to film and record your statement."

Liz put her hands up to her face. "You mean you need me to go through this again. Can't it wait until tomorrow?" She looked at her watch. "It's nearly five a.m. and I have to work this morning."

"I'd like to keep you at the station until I'm sure you're safe. Mick's murder is particularly gruesome. Killings like his are most usually personal, and of all the places he could have gone when he received parole, he came to Moonstone Lake. Furthermore, whoever murdered him could have killed him anywhere, but they chose to do it near your apartment. Until we know more, I have to assume you could be next."

Keith turned toward Liz's apartment. Jess called to him. "Do you want a tech with you?"

Keith kept walking. Nutmeg and I tagged slowly behind. He yelled back over his shoulder, "If I need one, I'll let you know. I don't expect to find anything up there."

Keith put his hand up to stop my progress. "Look at this." The stairs going up to Liz's apartment were red and smudged. "Didn't she say she didn't go upstairs?"

"Yes, that's what she said." I answered.

He stepped out of the doorway and called to *Jess*. "I was wrong. Have your guys search and you come with me. Bring your gear."

Liz Austin's apartment was upstairs from the Hoof and Mane Salon. If you didn't know about it, it would be difficult to find. The beauty shop faced the Boardwalk. The apartment was adjacent to Cobblestone Lane. Between each building a small path went from the front to the back. Because it was a tourist town, the narrow alleys were well lit and as clean as the streets. There wasn't any litter in Moonstone Lake. To make it harder to find, the door had, in hand painted letters, *Paper goods storage. Locker number 1242.*

Jess picked up a satchel and jogged over to us. I couldn't help but watch him. He had the body of a Navy Seal, the looks of a movie star, the smile of a toothpaste model and the personality of a good ole boy. "Oh my," he said as he stepped inside the tiny alcove at the bottom of the stairs. "That's a lot of blood. Let me go first. I'd like to get a head start on photos before anyone steps on it or touches the place." He turned his head to look back at us. "It isn't blood, it is paint. Smells like acrylic."

He took a camera from his bag and began to rapidly snap pictures of everything around him as he slowly climbed the stairs. Keith, Nutmeg and I waited at the bottom.

A minute or two later he called down to us. "Nobody's up here, but it is a mess. There is not a glass, paper, picture or drawer that hasn't been mutilated.

"I've seen a house after it's been searched, but nothing like this. They tore up everything."

I began to roam around. I heard a noise in the bathroom and tiptoed toward it. The water was on in the shower. The curtain lay in the tub and all of Liz's paints and brushes were in there with it. All of the paint tubes were squeezed and paint covered the walls. The items from the medicine cabinet were sunk under water in the sink. I backed out and called to Keith.

"Whatever this person or people wanted to find; they didn't care what they had to do to get it. First they killed a man and after that they destroyed an entire apartment."

Nutmeg whined and lay down behind the open apartment door.

Keith turned toward Jess. "Is someone trying to scare her? I'm glad she hasn't seen this. I wonder what Mick did in the years he has been gone from the area? Do you know Liz Austin?"

"Sure, we went to school together. I recognized her art work. Always was a talented gal."

I walked to look out the windows one by one and said over my shoulder. "Randy, Jess, Liz and I were in the same class. Mick was a year ahead of us."

"Isn't that unusual?" Keith asked.

"You mean all in the same class? Did you forget how small Moonstone Lake is without the tourists?" Jess patted Keith on the shoulder. You're not in Kansas anymore Dorothy. You're in Oz. We had one hundred and six kids in the school. That was from K through twelve."

"Our graduation class was a whopping eighteen kids. Four were tied for Valedictorian, including your red headed friend over there." He pointed to me. "Heck, until we were seven, we each went to one another's sleepover birthdays. Someone must have gotten smart because on my eight birthday Mom said *boys only* and I was devastated."

Keith looked from me to Jesse. "So did Mitch start with the rest of you, or transfer later?"

I answered. "I believe he was always with us, raising a ruckus and making enemies. I couldn't swear to it. I'll ask Mom, she knew everyone in the school and always offered to provide food for every occasion. If he ever had an event or gathering in this town, Mom would know his parents."

I remembered Liz's house from when we were in school. It was one of the largest and most beautiful homes in the area; and one of the most expensive. Her parents let her put her artwork all over it. The boat dock sported a flock of pink flamingos. They allowed her to paint an entire flower garden on the back of the house.

I remember it took her all summer to finish it. The house became a landmark. Visitors and tourists would drive by in their boats to see if she added anything new. All of the doors inside the house were painted with elaborate scenes. I remember a large elk painted on the door into her dad's den and a patch of sunflowers on the front door. It could have been gaudy but it didn't come off that way. Every year Moonstone Lake sponsored a Christmas house tour. The Austin's by far, got the most notoriety.

In high school Liz began to date Mick Dudley. It became the talk of the town. They were called *beauty and the beast*.

Her parents, who supported everything she did, wouldn't allow Mick in the house. In high school he spent more of his time in detention than he did in class. He joined the golf team in his junior year. The coach kicked him off when he lost his temper and threw his nine-iron into a pond on the Country Club course. There were many instances where he showed what an idiot he was, but now I could only recall one more. When he was a senior, he drove his car down the football field at a rival school because he didn't like their quarterback. We all thought going out with Mick was the way she rebelled against her parents. We all rebelled, but not as bad as Liz. Liz went to the Kansas City Art Institute and earned a degree in Visual and Art Design. I don't remember seeing Mick around while she was gone to school. When she came home, he showed up about six months later with a certificate showing he'd gone through a course to be a certified Nissan mechanic.

I don't think anyone was more surprised than Liz.

CHAPTER FOUR

Keith's cell phone rang and he answered it. "Really," he said, "and you're sure?" He listened for a long moment. "That would be great Casey. Can you send me a picture of the knife and one more thing? Why are her fingerprints on file?" He listened again. "Okay, thanks for the rush of the results."

Keith looked down and shook his head before he looked up at me. "There was only one set of fingerprints on the murder weapon. They belong to Liz Austin,"

I gave him a stern look. "She told me she pulled the knife out of his chest so she could give him CPR. I know she didn't kill him."

He gave me a flat-eyed look. "And why's that *Detective Summers*?"

"Because Nutmeg would not be so nice to her if

she killed someone."

He shook his head in disbelief. "Come on Ary. We all know the dog is smart, but that is a ridiculous statement."

I heard Nutmeg bound up the steps. She stood outside on the landing and growled at Keith. He looked at the dog and then back at me. He shook his head and took his phone out of his pocket.

He called Randy Malone. "Randy, where is Liz? Is she still at the jail with you?"

"No, I took her by her office where she had an extra set of clothes and then she got a room at Granny's Bed and Breakfast. What happened I don't know about?"

Keith answered. "Liz's fingerprints are the only ones on the murder weapon. Go over to her room and stay with her. Don't let her out of your sight."

"But Keith, when she gave me her statement, she said she removed the knife to help him. Maybe whoever actually killed him wore gloves."

I went into Liz's bedroom, packed her an overnight bag, retrieved her toiletries from the bathroom and handed the backpack to Keith.

I went to the top of the stairs, turned back toward him and said, "the bag is full of things to make Liz more comfortable while she's at Granny's.

Keith could be the most exasperating man, even a stranger knew Liz didn't kill Mick. He was in his detective mode; *the facts; just the facts.* Somehow, he forgot Liz, Randy and I were his best friends. We were his only friends. He'd only been in town for a little over a year.

I tried to look at the murder from his point of

view, a murder with a murder weapon and one set of fingerprints, the *proverbial smoking gun.* Some ideas were beyond comprehension. One was Liz having murdered someone. She always captured the spiders in her house and gently sat them outside. Not the actions of a murderer.

I looked at my phone. It was nearly ten. I'd be saved if Aunt Sandy got to work on time and my mother didn't order the staff to turn the buffet into a sushi bar in my tardiness.

It dawned on me as I walked the three blocks back to my apartment that I still had on sleepy shorts, an oversize tee shirt and nothing else. Oh my, I wasn't buxom, but I didn't go anywhere without a bra. On occasion, I shocked myself.

I went in through the front door of the apartment building. I didn't want to take the time to explain why I was late and why I wasn't dressed to anyone at the café.

I began to search my closet. Every week I told myself I wasn't too busy to clean my apartment and do my laundry, yet I didn't seem to get around to it until it was a crisis situation, like I had company coming to visit or there was not a thing to wear; literally.

I took a quick shower hoping the water would wake me up. I chose a comfortable mint green sundress with a square neck and shoulder straps and slipped it on over my head, lassoed my unruly and now wet hair in a ribbon, grabbed my sandals and headed downstairs toward the restaurant.

Aunt Sandy stood at the hostess table. I peeked around the corner and into the dining room. Usually by this time of day there were a few stragglers but the place had cleared out and we could all take a deep breath, wipe down the tables and trays, and clean the buffet before the lunch crowd arrived.

Although I rarely ate at other restaurants, because I deemed it a busman's holiday, when I did, I had my pet peeves. One was food and grime under the tables, next wet tables, and food all over the food bar. I also had the dish washer come out and put new serving utensils on the buffet every fifteen minutes because everyone who dines with us isn't a hand washer.

Aunt Sandy turned to greet me. "You look nice. Sleeping in must agree with you."

I gave her the condensed version of the events of the morning. She said nothing, only shook her head. We heard laughter coming from the dining room.

"Somebody's happy this morning," I said.

"It's Emma. She must have stayed up and baked all night. We walked in this morning to dozens and dozens of homemade cinnamon rolls dripping with icing. She has passed them out and has visited with the breakfast crowd since six."

I tiptoed to the edge of the wall and peeked around again. Mother came out of the kitchen with a tray of cinnamon rolls so large she had to carry it with both hands and leverage it against her big belly. Mom was in her element. She wore a vivid red full skirt. It hit her about two inches below her knee. Her blouse was a modest tailored long-sleeve white one with red collar and cuffs. The entire room looked at her as she twirled and swayed and put a roll on the table for each person.

She stopped in the center of the dining room. She had the crowd captivated with a story. For months mother's hair could only be described as Lucille Ball orange. Today her hair shined jet black and stuck straight up and out of a long red silk scarf to match the rest of her outfit.

She put the tray on a table and now had her hand tucked between her ample breasts and her belly. I couldn't tell if her hands were cold or if she was trying to hold the ladies up.

On anyone else the outfit might have looked ridiculous, but my eighty-year old mother had an air about her not seen on many people of any age. When folks saw her, they said, *that's Emma Summers.* It seemed to be enough to describe her.

Emma never met a stranger. The town loved her. She fed the poor, sponsored church events no matter what the denomination, and gave to band boosters, cheerleading camps, little league baseball and paid for funerals for the homeless. She was the main reason the café had survived over fifty years. We were complimented on the food and voted best place to eat in Moonstone Lake twelve years in a row.

When Emma stopped by a table to say hello, she made the diner feel like he was the only person in the restaurant. I'd been trying to convince her to come down once a day and walk around the dining room. The entire mood of the place changed when she paid a visit. Emma could get into more trouble than a pit bull on steroids. I thought maybe it would keep her busy.

I was the fifth generation to run Moonstone Lake Café and Sunday Brunch. The charter said the manager, on her seventieth birthday, must turn the restaurant over to her oldest daughter. Emma had enough money to own a home on the lake, have the biggest boat around and travel anywhere she desired. She chose to live in her apartment attached to the café.

Mom was the biggest control freak in the world. She was about to be eighty-one and I had been manager for going on eleven years. So far, we had kept our statis of best place to eat.

I shuddered to think what the story was she shared with them. I took a deep breath and smiled. Emma had no boundaries.

I looked toward the heavens and said a quick, *please don't let it be about me*, as I stepped into the room.

"There she is now," Mother announced when she spied me. The entire crowd broke into a series of applause, yells of *good job, and whistles*, and *you were such a lucky little girl*.

I knew my face was red; I could do nothing but smile and wave back. "Mom, may I speak to you in the kitchen?"

She held a now half empty tray of rolls, I took them from her and followed her as she sashayed, waved and smiled to her fans all the way out of the room.

I set the tray on the work counter and asked her. "Mom, what's the occasion?" Something frivolous I hoped.

"Arizona, I'm disappointed you don't know what day it is. Twenty-six years ago I flew to Phoenix and brought you home to be my daughter."

I looked at the floor. It took a long moment before I found the right words. It didn't take a genius to know the conversation could turn out badly. Ten times out of ten it did.

In the calmest voice I could muster I said. "Mother, you told the entire restaurant full of diners I am adopted?"

"Yes, honey, I did. I'm proud of you and I want everyone to know it."

"And you believe announcing to the world that I'm not your daughter will show you're proud of me, Emma?"

I often called her Emma. It began when I wanted her attention as a child and she didn't respond to Mom. "So now the entire town knows I'm adopted?"

"Yes, isn't it wonderful?" She pointed to the cinnamon rolls. "Want one? I know they're your favorite."

"Mom since you are so proud and happy about me, maybe this would be a good time to tell me why of the over four hundred thousand kids who wait to be adopted every year, you picked me out of all of them and flew over a thousand miles each way to bring me here?"

As usual when the subject arose, she clouded over and gave her standard answer. "It was a closed adoption. I don't know anything about your past. I don't want to talk about it. You should be grateful you live with people who love you. You own this popular restaurant and have never wanted for anything. That should be enough young lady. So much for celebrating your *Adoption Day*," she said as she turned and left through the kitchen's back door.

CHAPTER FIVE

I heard someone say in a loud voice, "Arizona, we need you." As I hurried toward the unpleasant raised voices, I saw Nutmeg. She stood near the front door to block an unkempt, short shaggy haired man in his early thirties from the dining room.

The man's camouflaged flak jacket was too heavy for our ninety-degree heat wave. He wore camo baggy pants three sizes too big. I doubted he'd had a bath in the recent past. If he moved an inch, Nutmeg bared her teeth and lunged toward him. She stayed far enough away from him as to not hurt him yet close enough to let the man know she meant business.

I had no idea what the problem was; I only knew I couldn't let my dog bite him. I commanded her. "Nutmeg. Nutmeg. Stand down."

Instead of the dog obeying as she always did, she took a step closer to the man and growled. The hair on the back of her neck stood straight up.

No diners could go out and none could come in. I walked up to Nutmeg and slipped my hand under her collar. I leaned down so we were eye to eye and asked her once again to back off.

Before she had time to react, Moonstone Lake's new lady police officer showed up, hand on her gun, and ordered the man to lay face down on the floor. When he didn't comply, Nutmeg stood at her full height and jumped on him. He fell over backwards and let out a string of words I would never repeat. Amanda reached around to her back and pulled out a pair of hand cuffs.

Two men, who happened to be at the cash register with Aunt Sandra, paying their checks, helped the man to his feet.

Amanda looked down at Nutmeg. "Thanks girl."

I walked up to stand next to my wonderful dog. "May I ask what your prisoner did?"

"He's been up and down the Boardwalk helping himself to a five-finger discount in each and every shop. He had an ice cream bar from Penguin's, beef jerky from the Smoke House and the latest best seller from The Plot Thickens. I'm guessing you were about to be taken for a meal."

I'd learned not to say *what else could go wrong*? Something could always go wrong,

I looked at the man, who I'd never seen before and told him. "Sir, if you are hungry, this restaurant will always provide food for you even if you can't pay for it."

Amanda smiled and said, "That's nice, Ary, but I doubt he's hungry. He likes the thrill of it. I've been one step behind him all day. He stole enough today to turn an infraction into a misdemeanor.

The rest of the day went off without a hitch. Since we are a café with a Sunday Brunch, we didn't have nightly specials. Our head chef, Louis, let me know how cost saving it would be if we added some. He said we would save countless hours in prep time. And how much food and hours we could save if we spotlighted one dish each night.

I said I'd try it, although I was apprehensive because the year before we put in a food bar. I hoped the idea wouldn't end up shooting us in the foot. The bar had been a hit and paid for itself in a few months. With Lewis track record it paid to listen to his ideas.

I took a seat at the service bar in the kitchen work area. Before he sat down, Louis poured us each a cold glass of tea, "Are you sure you want to put the food bar out to pasture?"

He patted a stack of magazines after he set them between us. "I've been reading industry magazines. They indicate there are two kinds of diners. There are the ones the older crowd frequent. Seniors are huge fans of daily specials. The specials are modestly priced, healthy and budgeted into the cost of eating here daily. It will get our seniors in here more than once a week when they realize they can't buy all the ingredients for the price of the nightly special."

"Are you sure we have enough seniors to make it profitable?"

He reached between the pages of one of the magazines and pulled out a single sheet of paper.

"This is a simple breakdown of the ages of our diners in the last month."

I took it from him. "How did you manage to do this?"

He smiled at me. "I've got friends outside the kitchen. I asked the servers if they would keep a tally. They were helpful, even Benny, the hardest working and fastest moving employee in the place took time to help me out,

"As you can see, the numbers are impressive. We have two times more seniors than the thirties crowd. The good thing about the senior's is most of them eat here year-round. The squatters inflate our numbers from the end of May to the first of September."

"Can I keep this paper? I get into so much trouble when I make these big changes without telling anyone."

He slid another piece of paper over to me. "Show them this. It is the list of specials along with a cost printout and how we plan to utilize the food bar." Louis stood, patted my hand and said, "I'd better get back to work. Let me know what you decide. Meanwhile, I'd better get the guys busy on lunch. It's beginning to fill up out there."

I turned around and looked into the part of the café I could see from my vantage point. "Thanks. I'll run it past Mom and Aunt Sandy as soon as I can."

I would wait a day or two. The last thing I intended to do for the next couple of days was to visit my mother.

He smiled at me. "Remember, you have the tie breaker vote." He flashed me his perfect Hollywood smile and went to work.

I was nearly out the door when he asked, "How is your friend, Liz? I'm sorry Mick is no longer breathing but I must say I didn't like the man."

"You and three quarters of the world," I said over my shoulder.

Chapter Six

The summer squatters were settled in. During the season Moonstone Lake's population ballooned from its normal twenty-two hundred inhabitants to well over six thousand.

None of the shop owners complained. The tourist's votes put The Boardwalk on the list of the five best places to vacation in the state and in the top fifty nationwide.

Almost immediately after I decided I was starving; I received a text from Keith. *I heard a rumor you have the best steak around. Got time for dinner?*

I text back; *Sure, but hurry, I'm starving. Tell me how you want your steak and we'll bypass the crowd.*

Keith walked into the dining room and I couldn't

help but swoon a bit. He stood over six feet tall, walked on the balls of his feet like a jungle cat and a had a tooth model's smile he flashed generously.

His every movement looked effortless. His black hair gleamed in the bright light. His eyes were so dark it was difficult to see where his iris left off and the pupil began. My heart beat a little faster as he came closer.

I blinked and changed my focus to Benny as he put the last of our food on the table of my booth at the far corner of the dining room. I never sat with my back to the café. I wanted to see who came and went.

Keith slipped into the booth facing me. "How's that for timing?" He picked up his steak knife but rather than cut his meat he held it up to examine it.

"Is there something wrong with the silverware?" I asked.

"No, not really, it doesn't seem like restaurant faire. It is bigger than any steak knife I've seen and I'm sitting here in amazement of its rosewood handle."

I stopped eating, put my elbows on the table, intertwined my fingers, rested my chin on them and looked at him. "Are you lacking conversational material tonight?"

He rested the knife on the edge of his plate and looked up. "I'm sorry, Ary, this is the same kind of knife we found next to Mick Dudley's body." He turned around to survey the room.

"Keith, eat your steak while it's hot. I doubt if the murderer is in here eating dinner."

He turned back to face me. "I'm sorry. I've eaten steak in a lot of restaurants and never before have I had it served with an expensive knife stuck in it. How common are these things?" He picked the knife up a second time and turned it over and over in his hands as if it were a rare coin.

"I'm not too well versed in how other places are run. Mother always says the most expensive meal in this café is steak and it should be special. We use these knives and pour a special mixture of garlic butter, and black pepper on the top of the meat immediately before it leaves the kitchen. The patrons rave about our steaks."

He began to eat. After a few bites he said, "I can see why they rave. How many of these knifes do you have?"

I smiled at him. "Keith, you will never find the killer if your only lead or clue is a restaurant steak knife. At one time we had around four hundred. With breakage and theft over the years, I would say we have about a hundred or so."

"Well," he said. "I think whoever killed Mick ate steak here."

I reached out and put my hand on his arm. "Keith, I would venture to say twenty-five thousand people have had access to these," I waved my knife at him, "in the last ten or fifteen years we have stocked them. Besides, Johnny's Steak House on the north side has the same style and brand. That brings your suspect pool up another ten or twenty thousand people.

"And seeing as the only finger prints are Liz's I'd bet the murderer wore gloves."

"Thanks, Ary, you're encouraging."

He frowned. "I interviewed her two friends.

Other than her finger prints and the blood all over her there is nothing else. The damage in her apartment pretty much excludes her as a suspect. Besides, Jess said the writing in the apartment was done by a southpaw. Liz is right-handed."

"Were there finger prints?"

"No. They used rags and brushes to do the damage. I believe it was well planned."

I leaned closer to him. "I'm glad you have decided it wasn't Liz. Honestly if Liz was going to kill him, I'd think she would have done it when he left her. Is she at the station?"

We stopped talking while Benny filled our water glasses. "Whoever killed Mick had to be strong enough to move him; or there is more than one person involved." I finished my salad as I thought.

We both knew Liz didn't kill him. The questions included who murdered him and what did he have worth killing for?

Keith grinned. "I hope we can find the body. The longer it is missing the more it deteriorates, the more clues are lost. Moving the body after death changes the lividity. It also will make it more difficult to pin down the time of death. Had it been there, we could have checked Liz's alibi with the time her friends dropped her off. This case would have moved smoother if she had only called from the crime scene."

"Another strange thing is when the CSI team arrived; all of the lights were on, the front alley light, the back one and the dawn to dusk over her apartment door."

"Maybe whoever killed Mick tried to muddy the

waters," I said.

Benny came to clear the table and offered us coffee and dessert. He smiled at me and added. "We have lots of cinnamon rolls. We are giving them away with every dinner."

I had to laugh in spite of myself. "Sure, Benny we'll take coffee and rolls. Warm them up for us please and make my coffee decaf." I focused my attention back on Keith. "How long will Liz be under police protection?"

"That's what I wanted to talk to you about. She stayed at Granny's last night but it isn't very secure if someone tries to get to her. The first night our police department picked up the bill. Now she is on her own.

"I think there is something *they* want and they believe she might have it. Otherwise they wouldn't have destroyed her apartment. I can't justify protective custody. No one hurt her, no one has followed her, and she hasn't had any communication with the killer or killers.

"The murderer made it clear though there is something of value. Could be anything. She might know, but if she does, she has forgotten it along with all the memories she put away. Mick Dudley must have been a piece of work.

"I know the apartment James lived in is still empty. It would be much more comfortable for her to stay there. She's afraid to go home. She couldn't if she wanted to. The girls at the salon called their insurance company and they gave an estimate of well over thirty-thousand dollars.

"Liz hasn't called her insurance company, but

she didn't have much left.

It is almost impossible for anyone to break into your place. I'll send a cruiser by several times a night in case anyone is hanging around. but I don't expect that to happen."

I looked up at him and shook my head. "I love Liz, she and I have been friends since kindergarten and yes, she can stay in the empty apartment. It still has the furniture in it."

CHAPTER SEVEN

I knew Mom and Aunt Sandy wouldn't mind if Liz stayed in the empty apartment but before she actually rented it, they needed to chime in. Years ago, my Grandmother bought the four plex between Granny's Bed and Breakfast and The Moonstone Café and Sunday Brunch.

Over the years we, meaning Mom, Grandma, Aunt Sandy and a couple of the café workers have lived there. Liz would be the first non-employee to move in. I had no idea what to charge her for rent.

Aunt Sandy sat on her stool at the front counter behind the cash register. I ran through a quick explanation of Liz's predicament. Her answer came with a smile. "Sure. And as far as the question of rent goes, charge her what she paid at her old apartment."

Mother lived on the first floor across from the

empty unit.

Noise from Mom's apartment radiated down the hall and assaulted my ears as I came in the back door. I knocked. "Mom, are you there?' This went on for a good five minutes. I reached down to open the door but she'd locked it. Next, I called her on her cellphone.

She answered on the sixth ring. "Hi, Arizona, what can I do for you?"

"Mom, you can turn down the noise and open the door. I need to talk to you."

"You wait right there, dear, I'll be right out. There's no need for you to come in, I'm very busy."

A lot of shuffling and laughter came from the other side of her door. It took her five minutes to come out. She squeezed between the door and the woodwork. She gave herself only enough room to come out sideways, one hefty leg at a time. "What is so important, young lady?"

I told my story about Liz one more time but with much more detail. Mother could ask a thousand questions about something not remotely important to the subject at hand.

This time she didn't ask one question or seem the least bit interested. When I told her what Aunt Sandy and I thought about the rent, she said. "Whatever you two decide on is fine with me."

As I walked away, I thought maybe there were aliens in her room. They did a personality and brain exchange. *Who was that woman and what have you done with my mom?* I shook the notion out of my head, smiled to myself and went to call Liz.

She answered on the first ring. "How's it going?

I'm sure Keith told you the apartment is open for you. You can either rent it or be a guest until you decide what you want to do.

"It's one of the safest places in town. If anyone tries to break in without the code, an alarm goes off at the police station. There are other safety features I can tell you about later."

She let out an audible sigh. "I'd love to rent it. During my lunch hour I went to my apartment to get a folder and the hair stood up on the back of my neck. I honestly don't think I could sleep there again, and I don't think I could ever look at those walls and not see the writing and paint everywhere. Am I being silly?"

I tried to calm her nerves. "I don't believe it's silly at all. No one knows who killed Mick or why. He, she or they might have known his ex-wife lived there or they might not. Sometimes our nerves try to tell us something. I'll meet you at the paper and we will get some of your belongings. Places don't seem as scary when someone is with you."

"You will? That's great. I have minimal furniture. They ruined my bed, sofa, the chairs and most of my paintings. They were mean enough to cut the backs off of all the pictures. Maybe whoever it was thought I had something hidden behind the paintings; like maybe the deed to a gold mine."

I tried to ease her mind. "I'm sure it is money or something valuable. Why else would he have mentioned money on his deathbed?

"We cleaned the apartment and all the furniture

after James left. There's a queen bed, couch, recliner, bookcase and a kitchen table and chairs. Oh, yes, there is a chest-of-drawers in the bedroom. All you need is bedding, towels and personal belongings and you're all set."

As I turned around to walk to the back to ask Benny if he could handle dinner without me, I ran smack into Randy. "Ary, just the person I wanted to see. Keith told me Liz was going to move into the empty apartment. I came by to tell you I'll offer my muscles and truck to help her move."

"That's great. Why didn't you call Liz?"

His face turned scarlet. "I didn't want to sound pushy. Can you tell her?"

I put both hands on my hips and smiled at him. "Randall Malone. You have a crush on Liz, don't you?"

I thought his face couldn't get any redder, but it did. "Come on Ary be a pal. Don't say anything to her. Too much is going on in her life. Besides, she's been single for years now.

"She hasn't shown an interest in anyone since Mick. I'd say he'd be enough to swear a woman off men. Sorry, I shouldn't have said that."

I put my hand on his shoulder. "I won't say anything. Is it possible for you to meet us at her apartment a little after five? We are going to move some of her belongings tonight."

"Sure, I'll be there." His Cheshire cat grin radiated and he turned and walked away whistling.

I stopped by the front of the café to visit with Aunt Sandy. "What's Randy so happy about?"

"Would you believe he likes our cooking?'

She sat on the edge of her stool, kicked off her shoe and bent her leg to rub the top of her foot. "Yes, I would but I doubt that's what it is. I haven't seen much of you lately. How are things going with the murder investigation?"

I called Nutmeg, who was in a corner, lying on her back with all four legs in the air, sound asleep. "I know. Maybe we should schedule a time for coffee or a glass of wine. I need a favor. Benny said he would close for me. I want to meet Liz and Randy at her apartment and help her move. She stayed at Granny's last night, courtesy of the police department. Tonight, she would have to rent a room."

She reached down and patted Nutmeg. "I don't have a problem with that. If you get done early enough, come by my apartment. I miss your smiling face."

"Will do," I said on my way out. "Love ya."

Before I left for the Moonstone Reflection I dropped by my apartment and changed into black rip-stop shorts, a light gray Moonstone Lake Café tee shirt and tennis shoes with no socks. I took time to wash my face, brush my teeth and gather my hair up into a pony tail."

Nutmeg and I jogged to the Reflection and arrived at the same time Liz stepped through the front door. The dog loved her and made three circles around her before she settled down to get his ears played with and a head rub.

We walked down the Boardwalk and between the buildings to Cobblestone Lane and Liz's apartment. We both stopped and stared at what we saw when we stepped out of the alley.

Keith and Randy had the tailgate of Randy's Ford-F150 pick-up down. They lounged on it drinking a beer. Keith wore bright red cargo shorts and a white body hugging Under Armor tee shirt. He didn't have an ounce of fat on him. When he first moved from the big city to Moonstone Lake, he had a bit of extra weight around his middle.

I stood there, crossed my arms and enjoyed the view. Liz didn't seem in any hurry to step forward either.

Randy had a wrestler's build. He stood two inches shorter than his boss and had a sturdier build. His sandy blond hair hung on his forehead but didn't quite fall in his eyes. He also wore shorts. He wore white with blue trim and his tee was blue with white lettering. It read POLICE. It reminded me of the Geranial's of my childhood.

Keith spotted us. "It's about time you two showed up."

"Isn't there an ordinance against public drinking?" I said with a smile.

They both jumped off the tailgate and met us half-way. "I didn't know you were going to help," I said to Keith.

He playfully pushed Randy's arm. "Randy said you needed muscle so I came."

We were able to put everything from the apartment into two truckloads. Once we began moving her belongings, we realized Liz had much more than she remembered. By the time we loaded and unloaded the truck twice we all collapsed in Liz's new living room.

I looked at my watch, "It's after ten. If it were

earlier, I'd have the kitchen send up a pizza."

"Not a problem," Randy said," I ordered from Pizza Hut a few minutes ago, one meat lovers, one cheese and an order of bread sticks and sauce." Randy, who had ten times more energy than I ran down the stairs to get the food when the buzzer went off.

Liz stood, walked into the kitchen and opened the fridge. "I don't really want a beer, but I'm really thirsty."

"Not a problem. I'll go to my apartment and grab some soft drinks and a bottle of wine."

Keith was on his feet in a flash. "I'll go with you. It sounds like another one of those chores requiring muscle."

When we got back, Randy and Liz had the pizza boxes open on the kitchen table. They each had a piece in their hand. Keith and I joined them.

We didn't talk about murder, Mick or work. Randy loved the St. Louis Cardinals and tried to make the three hour drive a few times in the summer to watch a game at the stadium. Keith followed the Chicago White Sox.

They compared National and American league pitchers and batting averages.

We devoured the pizza in no time. Liz piped up with, "Got anything sweet? I need enough energy to make my bed and find clothes for tomorrow."

I grabbed these while we were at my apartment. I opened a bag and shook out an array of candy bars. No one hesitated. We all ate one.

Keith and Randy stood and headed toward the sofa. "No, no, no," I said softly as they moseyed on.

Liz and I have real jobs and have to work tomorrow. We need to call it a night."

As if on cue Keith's phone rang. He hung up shortly. Randy and I have to go. Nobody told the Highway Patrol we don't have real jobs. We and a couple of the other guys are needed for traffic control out on Lake Road 91. I wish the squatters would learn no one can speed or drink and drive these roads and plan to make it home in one piece."

Randy looked down and raised his eyes to meet Liz's. "This is all going to work itself out. "

"Thanks for the help, guys. Ary and I would never have gotten this done."

In a move I would have considered too bold for Randy, he leaned down and kissed Liz on the cheek. Both of them blushed. Liz turned toward the bedroom and said, "I don't think this bed will make itself."

Randy walked out into the hall. Keith and I watched in stunned silence until Keith stepped forward and kissed me long and tenderly on the lips. "Thanks, Ary I had a great time tonight."

"So did I." I managed to squeak out.

I locked the door behind them and we headed back into the apartment.

Liz's place was the mirror image of Mother's. Sandy and I had the same set up upstairs."

We stopped at her door and she said goodnight.

"Are you sure you don't want my help with a few things. You must be exhausted and it wouldn't take ten minutes. You find something to wear tomorrow and I'll make up the bed. "

I helped and we had it all done in twenty

minutes. We said goodnight and I went upstairs to Aunt Sandy's place.

I stood outside her apartment door deciding if I'd wake her up if I knocked.

Before I could make up my mind, the door opened and there stood my aunt with a glass of wine in both hands. "I thought I heard the patter of little feet," she said as she looked down at Nutmeg and up at me "And the pounding of big feet."

I smiled, shook my head and took a glass of wine from her hand.

Sandy stood back and let us enter. Her three cats, Wynken, Blyken, and Nod were asleep on the couch until they saw Nutmeg.

All three of them jumped down and began weaving in and out of her legs. They purred so loud we could hear them clearly from the kitchen.

I sat and turned back to watch as Nutmeg plopped down, rolled over and let the three of them walk all over her. She playfully batted at them with her paws and in returned they kneaded their paws on her belly.

My Aunt Sandy's apartment was all things cat. The number three on her apartment door was on the back of a tabby cat Liz painted one year for her birthday. The light switches were replaced with porcelain cats. The dish towels looked like images of her three, Wynken had shining black hair with a perfect tuxedo on his chest. Blynken's vivid orange fur reminded me of a sunset, and Nod, leader of the pack, a classic calico with a black spot over one eye and a tan one over the other was my favorite.

Aunt Sandy's voice brought me back to the

present. "Did you get Liz moved in?"

"We did. Keith and Randy helped. It's been a long time since I've spent and evening with people my own age. It was fun and the men did the heavy lifting."

"Both of them helped? Do I smell romance in the air between Randy and Liz?"

I smiled. "He admitted to me earlier today he had a crush but said he wouldn't act on it because he believed Mick ruined her from ever wanting another relationship."

Sandy went to the refrigerator. "Never say never. Are you hungry?

"No, between us we ate enough pizza to feed a family of eight. I need to go to bed. I'm supposed to open tomorrow so Abby can try out for a part in the community Christmas play. We'll all be glad when she's done and we don't have to listen to a line from it every time we see her.

"And why do they begin practice so early in the year? It isn't even August."

I stood, brought my hands up to my face in a praying gesture and said, *don't yawl just love this snow. When it snows on Christmas, there is magic in the air."*

We both laughed. I stood to signal I needed to go home and go to bed.

"Don't run off," she said. I need to talk to you about your mother."

"… and your sister. Now what it she up to?"

"I'm not sure. She says it's a Parcheesi Tournament. This morning UPS delivered a fold up card table and four folding chairs; the second one this week.

"When she came down to let the driver in, I asked why she needed another table. She said, *the folks at the senior center heard about her tournament and began to join us. I may need two more."*

"I have a big problem believing Arial Steiner, Margie Gold, Jake Wilson, Johnny Cake; I never did know his real name, and Mary Johnston who are all well over eighty are coming and going at all hours of the day and night for a board game. There is more going on there than she wants us to know."

I took a step back into the room. "Actually, you might be right. When I called to tell her I was coming up to talk to her about renting James' apartment to Liz, she said don't come. She was hungry and would meet me in the dining room. I didn't think anything about it at the time. I went to her apartment anyway and she wouldn't let me in. She opened the door enough to let a leg slip through and quickly closed it."

"I believe it is time we pushed a little harder to find out what she is up to."

"Actually, you might be right. We can check off immoral, they are all too old. We can check off an exercise group. The collective weight of the people we know are up there is at least eighteen hundred pounds. If they had an exercise routine going, we would be able to hear it in the kitchen."

Nutmeg stood and all three cats tumbled to the floor. She shook and came to sit beside me. She whined, something she never did, sat back on her haunches and covered her eyes with both paws. "Thanks Nutmeg," Sandra petted the top of her head. "If we go by what your very talented, sweet, dog has to say, it isn't good."

CHAPTER EIGHT

Around midnight a storm blew in from the southeast. The rain beat down, lightning flashed and thunder rumbled across the sky. On a normal night I could sleep and storms didn't bother me. On this night the wind howled and tornado alerts went off at various times during the wee hours of the morning.

I woke up more tired than when I went to bed. Outside the sun shined, no breeze stirred and the way the air conditioner hummed hour after hour, I knew the summer heat had found Moonstone Lake.

Rain, heat, humidity, or snow and ice didn't keep me from my morning jog. Nutmeg on the other hand let me know if she didn't have to protect me, she would as soon lay on the cool sidewalk and take a nap.

I tried to hurry her along so I would not be late

for work. I had not made it to work on time the last five days. Good thing I was boss, otherwise I might be unemployed.

A man lounged on a bench near the jogging track. I lived in town most of my life and I knew the bench where he sat should have faced the other direction. The muddy mess and footprints in the area proved me right. He moved it so he could clearly see the front of our apartments.

Immediately I thought of Liz and Mick. The hair stood up on the back of my neck. Could he be watching Liz or did it have something to do with my mother's strange behavior of late.

I ran as far as I could in my usual direction and the man didn't move. I turned and ran back toward where I began.

Nutmeg passed by him each time I did and didn't react or act as if she noticed him. Keith thinks I'm daft when I say this, but if the man had evil in his heart, Nutmeg would have warned me.

When I arrived back at my apartment, I looked out the window and the man had turned the bench around and I didn't see him anywhere.

I wrote down every detail I could remember. Six feet tall, shaggy brown hair, cargo shorts, Nike tennis shoes, athletic build. I knew him to be right-handed because he worked a crossword puzzle. Whether he was good looking or not was subjective, but I gave him an eight.

I thought about him as I showered and dressed for work. I knew I should call Keith, but since the man didn't do anything other than to sit in a different direction on a wooden bench and make footprints in the rain-soaked soil, I filed the incident away for later. I *put it on the back burner* as my mother would say.

When I went to my closet to find an outfit, I smiled. For three days I kept my clothes picked up, returned all my dirty dishes to the café kitchen and made my bed. My all-time record was ten days.

I loved to wear shorts to work but I had to be careful they touched the top of my knee as not to draw criticism from the older set, including Mom and Aunt Sandy. This day I chose white Bermuda shorts, an orchid button up shirt with darker flowers and Teva sandals. I looked myself over. No one could complain about me yet today my brain added. The little red headed girl from the orphanage.

I had a flash of a young woman with a wide-eyed smile and a soft voice. The image left as quickly as it came. I went to the living room and looked out the front window. Try as I might, there was nothing else.

My goal was to drop in downstairs, make sure the café didn't have any problems and then talk to Mother. My plans changed when I walked in and she sat at a table in the center of the room eating breakfast. I glanced at my watch. It was a little after eight a.m.

I went to join her. "Hi Mom. How's the Parcheesi tournament going?"

"Do you mean my Rook Tournament?"

"Sorry. Aunt Sandy told me Parcheesi."

She looked up from a plate of bacon, eggs, country fries with brown gravy and a separate plate of three pancakes. "My sister is confused. Would you like to join me? You are much too skinny."

Stan came over with a coffee and turned my cup over to fill it, "Can I get you some breakfast, Ary?"

Mother looked up and glared at me. She thought I let the people who worked for us get too familiar. When she ran the restaurant, she demanded to be called Mrs. Summers. She said if line between help and staff remained friendly, yet well-defined, would help when you needed a job done no one wanted to do. No way I had or would tell her I did most of those myself.

The crew I had were loyal to me. They attended college or had young children. I knew a few of them came to the restaurant exhausted and left the same way. Every day I provided a meal before their shift if they wanted to come in for it, I made sure everyone had an uninterrupted thirty minutes during their shift to do what they wanted. Some made phone calls, others ate, some studied and once in a while I would find someone asleep on a bench behind the café.

I smiled at Mom and ordered French toast with strawberries and whipped cream. "How does your Rook tournament work? Can I drop in and play?"

Her head shot up and she eyed me as though I were a stranger. "Absolutely not, I mean, we have the roster filled out for the entire event. You don't have time to play anyway. You might have to play hours at a time if you win. I believe it would be best if you find another hobby. And besides Ary; let's be honest. You don't really like my friends."

She pushed her plate away and looked at me over her half glasses. "We begin at ten. I don't want to be late."

As she sauntered out the door, I noticed she

didn't have shoes on. Her rainbow-colored pants fit better than most things she tried to make into her style. Her top had a Latin American look. The neck line plunged a little but the effect was less noticeable due to small rows of ruffles that circled it in the same pattern as the skirt. I heard her hum as she opened the door to the apartments.

Mom left before my food came. I motioned back to my usual booth and Stan took my food there. I didn't realize how hungry I was until I smelled the aroma of the warm fresh French toast in front of me.

Someone slid into the other side of the booth. It was Randy Malone. "Hi, this is a pleasant surprise," I said.

He laid a manila envelope on the table and slid it toward me. "I'm sorry about this, Ary."

I looked at his troubled face and down to the envelope. "Is this for me?"

"Not really," he said, "but I didn't want to do anything until I talked to you"

Reluctantly, I opened it. It began, *To Whom It May Concern,* the first few pages were a search warrant for Emma Jean Summer's apartment. It stated they were looking for illegal gambling paraphernalia and ill-gotten gains from illegal gambling and in other words I wouldn't have understood without a law degree.

The next four or five pages were entitled *Probable Cause Statements.* It listed times of people's coming and goings from Mother's apartment and the names of five people who were contacted and verified the complaint. A separate document said Mother had to surrender herself under a charge of running an illegal gambling game from her place of residence. Any and all paraphernalia, ill-gotten gains and props would become the property of the county until the case was settled.

I looked at Randy who studied me intently. "I'm sorry, Ary. We had no other choice. Seems one of her friends lost his entire pay check playing Texas Hold'em at your mom's and his wife instigated the complaint.

"We might have been able to do this quietly but his Mrs. bypassed us locals and went straight to the State Attorney's Office. It took a while for the entire case to filter down to us."

I put my hand on his. "This is not your fault. She told her sister it was a Parcheesi tournament and me they played Rook. She hasn't caused any trouble down here in at least a month. I read a section of the papers out loud to Randy. What's this about food?"

"Riley Durum, who signed the complaint, said Emma sold snacks every night. She has her chef fix them which could put the restaurant in jeopardy.

"Lewis gave his statement to Amanda a minute ago. He said he didn't know she sold the food. He said he feeds all of you when you're not at work and regularly provides food for parties and get-togethers."

"It doesn't make the lot of us seem self-reliant does it? Where is Keith?" I asked.

"He drove to the Ozark Correctional Prison to interview the men who served in prison with Mick Dudley. He said to tell you he'd talk to you when he gets back."

So much for breakfast, my appetite turned to

butterflies as my food turned cold. Amanda came up to us. She slid in next to Randy. "I'm here to help. We would like for no one to leave your mom's apartment before we interview them. I believe your mom will be more comfortable with me going through her personal belongings rather than Randy."

They slid out of the booth. I gazed toward them. "Should I go with you?"

Both of them shook their heads. "No, it is best if you stay out of this. Your mom will need an ally and it would be difficult for you if you're there when we take her in."

"So, what should I do?"

"You could let us in the main door so we don't have to damage anything. Do you know the five-digit code to open her apartment door?"

"No, I don't. The best I can do is let you in the front door or the back. Is there any way you could take her out through the kitchen without handcuffs?"

"Ary, you know I'll do the best I can to keep this low key. These searches take forever. We have to log every item we take with us and interview the players who are in the apartment now.

"As soon as we go upstairs, go on with life as though you don't know about this. Wait until you get a call from the station."

"You mean you are taking her to jail?" I didn't expect an answer. I walked them to the pass-through door and pressed the key pad.

Randy touched my arm and Amanda smiled at me. "It is not your fault. Try to relax. There's nothing you can do right now. I seriously doubt they will throw the book at a bunch of octogenarians for playing poker. The judge will fine her and give her a slap on the wrist. I think what we are doing now is only because the lady who wrote the complaint went to the States Attorney General instead of her local authorities.

CHAPTER NINE

I looked around the dining room. It buzzed along like the well-oiled machine it was. I took a few minutes to go outside and sit on the bench under the Hackberry tree in front of the apartments. I wanted a moment to catch my breath.

Sometimes Mom acted more like a rebellious teenager than a retired soon to be eighty-one-year-old.

Hours past and no word came from Randy, Amanda or Keith about Mom. I told myself she was small potatoes compared to the rest of their cases.

I compartmentalized her ordeal for as long as I could. I desperately wanted to know how the arrest went and if the judge thought it necessary to lock her up. I couldn't wrap my head around any of it. Whose eighty-year old mother gets arrested for running a poker game in her home?

I tried to find some humor in the situation but I couldn't.

If I ever needed to be arrested, I wanted Randy Malone to do it. He was kind, gentle, and understanding. The look on his face said it all. He didn't want to be the one who had to arrest my mother.

Lunch ran so long it bumped into dinner. Ham and beans and cornbread night brought out half the town. It seemed to be a hit especially with the squatters. Mom and Aunt Sandy cringed when I called the summer tourists squatters, but they were.

They invaded Moonstone Lake around Memorial Day and stayed until Labor Day. The settlers came in covered wagons; squatters came in SUV's and Lexus'. Everyone had some sort of watercraft. Those with smaller boats pulled them down every year. Folks with bigger rigs rented marina space and left them at the lake all winter.

Each year the young locals who worked on and about the lake for summer jobs, uncovered the boats, cleaned them, and gassed them up.

Every store and restaurant in the entire town upped their inventory and stocked more items popular with city folk than lake folk. All in all, it was mutually beneficial for all involved. Most of the families came every year.

They were around when I grew up and I watched their families grow, the children go off to college and get married, the old people dropped off and babies were born.

Some I truly liked; others treated us more like

servants than equals.

I learned the lesson early in life. Mom and Aunt Sandy told me at least a hundred times a summer to play with my own friends. Don't get too friendly. No matter what these people say or do, they are leaving in September.

Over the years I saw young couples, one from the lake and one from the city have summer flings. When push came to shove, each went his separate way in the fall. They promised to write and stay true until the next season. For the most part, they forgot one another within a week.

Considering four thousand different personalities overflowed the town, we had very little trouble.

A noise woke me from my stupor and I headed back to work. I strolled around the food bar, checked the soft serve machine. I noticed the corn bread was the most popular.

I went into the kitchen to chat with Lewis. "What are you doing to the cornbread? Bobby has filled the bin five times in the last hour. I have never seen anything move so fast."

"I added a can of creamed corn to each batch. The crowd loves it. I hadn't made cornbread for so long I forgot how much better it tastes with corn added. Here, try a piece; it's warm, and fresh out of the oven. I'll put some butter and honey on it."

"You amaze me, Lewis. You are one of the main reasons this place is a success."

He pointed toward the stools on the other side of the work station. "Have a seat. I'll serve you some of our fabulous ham and beans and listen to you compliment me some more."

Mother's ordeal killed my appetite at breakfast. The lunch mad house kept me running all afternoon. Now the dinner crowd filled the diner. It promised to be a big night.

"I didn't realize how hungry I was until you mentioned it. I need to talk to you. Do you have time to join me?"

"I always have time for you, Arizona. How can I help you?" Lewis stood over six feet. For a man in his sixties he moved lightly on his feet. His dark skin stood out under a white chef's smock and his salt and pepper hair and twinkling eyes made him appealing.

I couldn't help but smile. "Mother's at it again. This time she is in jail for it. I'll go fetch her after we close, but it wouldn't hurt for her to stew for an hour or so. The truth is, I'm a bit worried, it's been hours and hours since they went to her room."

He sat on a stool across from me. "Amanda brought her through here about two hours ago. Emma didn't look my way.

"In the twenty years I've been here I thought she had done everything. What is it this time? Officer Amanda dropped by early this morning and questioned me about how much and how often I send food to Emma's apartment. I knew she had been up to something but I couldn't lie for her."

"She has been running a poker game for wayward retirees. And, she sold all the food you made to the players. How long have you provided snacks for her?"

He tried to keep the smile off his face but he couldn't. He shook his head. "It's been over a month. I'm not out anything. I did all of it when I was on the clock and it wasn't my food. Where is she?"

"The police arrested her this morning. She broke several laws."

"Must have been where Amanda took her earlier. I can't imagine your mother with an orange jumpsuit," he said.

I began to clean my plates but he stopped me. "I'll do that. You go bail out our own *Ma Barker.*"

Chapter Ten

When the restaurant closed Nutmeg and I jogged to the end of the Boardwalk. The police station sat on the west end. They said not to come until they notified me, but after all, she was my mother and she was eighty.

Amanda Wade had front desk duty. I could see Keith in his office. He looked up when he heard me in the lobby and came out to the hall to greet me. "Hi. We need to talk."

Nutmeg and I followed him. I sat in the chair he provided for visitors and my dog sat near the door.

Keith took a notepad out of his drawer and put it in front of him. "What do you want to talk about first, your mother or Mick Dudley's murder?"

"Where *is* my mother?"

"She is in jail. I'm sorry, Ary, there was nothing I

could do. Judge Rand saw her earlier, advised her of the charges against her, set bail and suggested she hire an attorney."

"So, this is serious." I said.

"It could be. I think she can most likely settle out of court. He set bail at five thousand dollars. You'll need ten percent of it to spring her. She told the judge she didn't know gambling in her own home was against the law. I doubt he believed her. He said it didn't matter if she knew it was wrong or not, *ignorance of the law is not a defense* "

I shook my head. "What about her friends? Are they in trouble?"

"The judge had her write the names of everyone involved and then told her she needed to stay at least one hundred yards away from them until this is settled.

"There are eleven of them involved. Judge Rand sent Amanda and Randy out to serve them with summons to appear papers. He set the hearing for two weeks from tomorrow. They will each be fined but no jail time.

"I bet her buddies try to guilt her into paying their fines. I guess there is no honor among octogenarian gamblers."

"Geez, Keith, she really did it this time. Can they do that; make her pay their fines I mean?"

He leaned back in his chair, clasped his hands behind his head and gave me a big smile. "No, she didn't kidnap them and make them go to her apartment and gamble. The ones who have checked in so far are more afraid of their spouses and your mother than they are the judge.

"Jake Wilson's wife told me he would say he needed to run an errand and not come back for hours. When she questioned him about what took him so long, he said he ran into an old friend. The entire ordeal raised her suspicions.

"She followed him and found out what was going on. She gave him what for but instead of coming here, she called the Attorney General. It's why this small thing turned into a big thing."

I couldn't hold my anger any longer. "I swear, Keith, it is like I have a five-year-old. If a small child is quiet for too long, you need to check on what they are up to. Mother is the same way. Tell me what I need to do."

I could tell he hated to be in a situation where he had to be a part of arresting my mother. "If you have five hundred dollars lying around, you can write a check and they will let her go until the case goes to court or the matter is settled. If you don't have the cash you can put an item of equal value up for collateral. The downside to all of this is the county clerk works from seven in the morning until three in the afternoon which means your mom can't be released until morning."

I shook my head and said out loud what I meant to keep to myself. "She ran the café for sixty-seven years. Maybe she is having her childhood now. Aunt Sandy and I have tried over the last several years to encourage her to go somewhere, do something."

I glanced up at Keith's face. I couldn't read it, but I guessed he wouldn't want to hear about my rebel-rouser mom's escapades.

He took my pause as an opportunity to steer the

conversation back to the problem at hand. "Even if you wanted to bail her out tonight you couldn't. Do you want to see her?"

"No, since I can't do anything tonight, I think I will leave her where she is. Should I picture her on a thin mattress with no pillow or blanket and a bucket in the middle of the floor for sanitation?"

He laughed and walked around the desk toward me. "She will be okay where she is. Randy put her in the holding cell downstairs near the offices. He gave her a blanket and pillow and ordered her dinner from Bueno Taco, last I heard, she was snoring. "

I walked out in front of him. "I love my mother, but there would not be a reason I could give her that would justify why I couldn't spring her tonight."

We stood in silence. "I went to Fordland today and talked to Mick Dudley's supposed cell mates."

I walked toward a bench and sat down. "Don't keep me in suspense. Did you learn anything?"

"Lots. First the warden told me he never actually had Mitchell Dudley in his custody. Since the man is dead, he let me see the papers he was sent from the Supreme Court of Indiana.

"Mitchell Dudley was to be given the prisoner number of OWF 117965. He said the OWF was supposed to stand for Ozarks Work Farm.

"He always thought Mick was moved to witness protection, but the U.S. Rangers handle the WPP so I eliminated it as an option as to where he went for five years or why he was set free. My next step would be to talk to the coroner and reread the autopsy report. For that I would need a body. I need to find out what the court fiasco here was about. The entire ordeal is mind boggling.

"I know Liz is afraid and I hate to talk to her again. She must have had a few clues as to who he was and where he has been, even if she doesn't know it."

CHAPTER ELEVEN

Business had nearly doubled. We couldn't keep up with the number of diners without hiring more staff. I put an ad in the Reflection and went down to the restaurant early to conduct some interviews.

I hired the last new worker late in the morning. We now had two new servers and a new line cook. They would start in the morning.

I had plans to put the new hires with a couple of seasoned workers for the first few days.

I knew both of the girls. One ran cross country at the high school. Since it was my sport, I followed it religiously. The other girl's mother was a nail tech at the Hoof and Mane. I'd seen her when she was younger and worked as the shampoo girl at the salon.

Liz walked up behind me as I poured a cup of coffee. "Want one?" I said when I saw her in my peripheral vision.

"Sure," she said. I handed her an empty cup. She poured her own and began to add cream. Her hands shook so badly she spilled some.

I headed to my usual booth and she followed. "Are you okay?"

She slipped onto the bench across from me. "Not really. I think someone is following me."

"Any idea who? What's he look like? Did you call Keith?" I asked all in rapid succession.

She raised both hands and said, "Jeez, Ary, all these questions are making me dizzy."

"I'm sorry, truly I am. Tell me what is going on."

Liz leaned back against the bench and took several deep breaths. "Someone's following me. There's not much more to tell. It can't be a coincidence the same man window shops behind me everywhere I go.

"I stopped by Bueno Taco to pick up lunch for the office. A man followed me inside, took a seat at the back table, but he didn't order anything. He left when I did. I saw him again, just now. He was across the street from the newspaper when I came out. I saw him twice more before I got here."

I looked around the café, as if I thought I might see someone out of place. I smiled at Liz, hoping she didn't think I was as silly as I felt at the moment. "What does he look like?"

"He's about six feet, nice build, brown shaggy hair. His hair sticks out around the band of his Nike ball cap.

He wears the hat down low and the bill shades most of his face. One reason he stands out is because he has on long pants and a light-yellow windbreaker. Last time I looked; the temperature was well over ninety."

"Jeez Liz, I'd be afraid. Tell me you told Keith," I said.

"I sent Keith a text, but he hasn't answered. Ary, I'm really scared."

As if on cue, Keith walked in, looked around, saw us, came to the booth and slid in next to me. "I got here as soon as I could. Randy stopped the man in question. He's harmless. He's a relative of one of the families on the back side of the lake. Name is Roy. He's an odd guy, but he didn't kill Mick or mean to scare you. They don't usually let him wander around alone. This is the fourth year they have come here for the summer.

"The entire family was out looking for him. When you texted me, Randy had already told me we had a missing eighteen-year-old autistic man wandering the streets. His family said he hangs out on Drop Rock pier from morning to night. They had no idea he wasn't there."

Liz looked relieved. "Where are we on the murder?"

Keith told Liz all the facts he gave me the evening before. I noticed he didn't take his eyes off of her. If he wanted to gage her reaction, I only saw surprise and shock.

"So, we may never know who killed Mick or why or who he actually was."

Keith looked at me and then Liz. If you two have time for lunch I'll tell you what I think."

We both agreed to lunch, we ordered three

cheeseburgers; loaded, three orders of onion rings, two cokes and an ice tea.

The food arrived and I said to Keith, "Let's hear your theory."

"I think he came into some money. I don't know why or how much. He was safe here until five years ago when somehow, he was spotted. The authorities moved him again. I don't know if he got tired of the hiding or just wanted to come home.

"Someone was watching Moonstone Lake and when he came back here, they killed him.

"I don't know the *whys* yet. I'll call Chief Chase in the morning. Now that I know he wasn't arrested and put in jail, and he is dead, maybe they won't have to keep the secret any longer."

Liz's hands began to shake again. She held a French fry and put it back on the plate. "This is all scary to me. Can you imagine living with a man who was whisked off to a secret place? I don't understand why he never told me. Between high school and our marriage, I know there were times he could have confided in me."

Keith downed the rest of his ice tea. "Maybe he didn't know. How much do you remember about his family? Was he an only child? What were his parents like?"

Liz scooted out of the booth. "I need to think. I am the kind of person who goes on. I rarely look back. My parents were killed. I was on tenuous terms with them because of my relationship with Mick.

"I had to stop thinking about what might have been or what could be and went with what is.

"I'm going back to work. I might not be best

friends with everyone there, but I believe they are normal." She took her purse and turned to leave. "I need normal"

I walked Keith to the door. Nutmeg came out from her hiding space and slipped out the door. She caught up with us outside. Keith stopped to pet her. I poked him on the arm and said, "Liz didn't get very far. She sat on the bench under the Hackberry tree and stared out into space. We walked over to her. Nutmeg jumped up on the bench and sat next to her with her head in Liz's lap.

Keith said, "let's go to Danny's, sit in the garden and relax. We've had a long week.

He turned back to the café. "Ary, you could use a break from all of this. And Liz, you need to do something besides think of Mick's murder every minute. I'll let Randy know. No way will you be in any danger with two cops along."

We agreed to meet at nine. I had to close the restaurant. I had told Aunt Sandy and Benny I'd close for them. They each had plans

Chapter Twelve

The time had come. I had to face my mother. I wrote a check for five hundred dollars from her account. I didn't look forward to the next few hours.

As Nutmeg and I jogged toward the county jail. I smiled. I never thought the words *bail my mother out of jail* would ever cross my lips.

Her birthday loomed down on me. I needed to defuse the situation with her friends. The entire town came to the café on her birthday. We served free birthday cake and food. Any money we lost on Mom's birthday, we earned back in good will.

I had ten days to smooth out the problems with her buddies, go over a menu with Lewis, and put a birthday notice in the newspaper.

We started with her retirement party on her birthday when she turned seventy-five and had a get together every year since. Mom liked nothing better than to be center of attention for an entire day.

I arrived at the jail early afternoon and realized I didn't drive the car. Although it would be good for her, I doubted Mother would want to walk six blocks home.

I took care of the paper work in the county clerk's office and waited while a guard escorted Mother from the jail to the court house.

It was an ordeal to pay the bail. First, she had a fit about the amount and secondly, she didn't want to sign the release papers.

They stated she couldn't leave the county until the case was resolved. Why she made such a fuss, I'm not sure. She hadn't left the county in five years. The other stipulation said she could not have any contact with the eleven friends who were in the gambling *incident* as they called it.

She let them know they were ruining her social life. She changed her tune when she was told all of them had filed lawsuits against her.

Once she found out her friends *betrayed* her, as she put it, she didn't say another word. To my surprise she petted Nutmeg when she saw her and said *she'd love to walk home.*

Mom put her palms on her face and with more drama than I'd seen on a movie screen said, "I haven't had any fresh air since I was arrested. What a way to treat the elderly."

Our walk turned out to be pleasant. We stopped at Penguin's and bought rocky road ice cream cones, her favorite.

No sooner did she see her apartment than her

mood changed. She harrumphed and crossed her arms over her chest. "Arizona, you sure took your time coming to get me. I guess you think the entire ordeal is funny."

I glanced toward her. "I came last night but they don't have a clerk after five pm so I had to leave you until today. Keith said you were fine."

Mom didn't go into the café; she went straight to the front door and punched the numbers on the keypad so hard I thought it would break. She turned around, glared at me as if I were the enemy and disappeared inside.

Nutmeg stepped closer to my leg, sat, and extended her paw to shake my hand. What a great dog.

I had an appointment with Lewis. He looked up when I entered the kitchen. "Emma wants Sandy to bring some dinner to her. She says she hasn't eaten since yesterday morning."

I smiled at him. "Dramatic, isn't she? I'm sure they fed her, they just didn't' feed her anything she liked. Did she say what she wanted?"

"No, she said *whatever we can spare.*"

"I'll tell Aunt Sandy. She'll be back to get a tray a little later. How long do you need to put something together?"

"Should I feed her the special?"

"Sure, she likes roast beef, mashed potatoes, gravy and veggies. Add a gooey dessert and a side salad."

Aunt Sandy stood at the hostess podium and grinned at me as I walked up. "How's our jailbird?"

"Don't say that to her. She sees no humor in it.

She was even more upset when she found out I took the money from her personal account and not mine or the restaurant's. I never dreamed I'd have a juvenile delinquent on my hands at this time in my life."

I perched on the edge of the stool next to her.

She looked up at me. "I haven't talked to you in ages. I miss the nightly visits and the cats miss Nutmeg. Think you can come by tonight?" She asked.

"Randy, Keith, Liz and I are going to Danny's. Come along. It's not dates, just friends. They would love it."

"Oh, honey. Your feet are twenty-five years younger than mine. I'm going to the book store to pick up the newest Karin Slaughter novel and then to my easy chair to put my feet up."

I stood, walked behind her and rubbed her shoulders. "Okay, old lady. I'll stop by if we aren't out late."

"Good, did you remember tomorrow night is book club? I don't see Emma going and if you don't show up there would be five of us at the most. It's at Julie Sanborn's house. We both know the preparation it takes to be hostess."

I looked down at my feet and back to Aunt Sandy. "Geez, I forgot all about it. I didn't even open the book and I forgot to tell Lewis we need a dish for tomorrow night."

"Don't worry about it. I'll ask Lewis, he won't mind and when you come by tonight, I'll fill you in on the story line of the book. It will all work out."

Benny interrupted us to give Aunt Sandy a dinner

tray for Mom.

I smiled at my aunt and best friend. "You'll have to take it. She's angry with me for not springing her sooner." I surveyed the dining room. We were between lunch and dinner. There were five people in the entire dining room.

Sandy looked down at the tray. "So, you are going to throw me to the wolves? You know how upset she gets. She can rationalize anything in her favor." As though resigned to her chore, Sandy picked up the tray, walked to the pass-through door, glanced back, gave Benny and me a big smile and disappeared.

The rest of the day went smoothly. No one complained about their dinner and everyone in the place behaved as if it were a holiday.

I left the restaurant in Louis' capable hands. Riley Durham took over the cashier's chores for Aunt Sandy. Louis offered to put the money in the safe. We could count the receipts in the morning

I went to my apartment to shower and change clothes. I picked out a teal colored cotton tank and a short pale-yellow skirt. I slipped on blue flip flops and brushed my hair into a ponytail.

Mom always told me if I wanted to make the lightest color in my outfit show up, I should wear an accessory the color I wanted to bring to the forefront. In this case I chose a pair of medium yellow wrapped paper earrings made in Rwanda and a pale-yellow scarf.

A glance in the mirror reminded me no matter what I wore, the most predominate color on me would always be my red hair.

I didn't wear a watch but my phone screen flashed

eight-thirty. On my way downstairs to the outside door, I stopped by Liz's apartment to see if she wanted to walk with Nutmeg and me to meet the guys.

There was no answer. I peeked into the restaurant and asked Amanda, who manned the hostess table, if she'd seen Liz. She said no.

"Come on Nutmeg." I coaxed my beautiful, shaggy, four-legged friend. "We didn't make plans for her to walk with us. She is most likely already there and sipping her first glass of wine."

. Nutmeg and I headed down the street.

A full moon hung low over the lake. It lit the entire area as twilight lingered and the still setting sun cast light on it and turned it blood red. Light cascaded across the lake in magnificent hues of orange and a bit of purple and yellow. I couldn't help but stop to stare.

Lovers, friends and families filled the parks, fished, rode in boats and wave runners; a true Saturday Evening Post cover.

The Hug a Mug Coffee Shop had a waiting line as did Penguin's Frozen Treats. The Boardwalk was such you could walk in the street. A large archway made of vines blocked off one end and the other had a building where one could buy tickets for a ride around the lake in a three-decker boat to see the beautiful houses built on its shores.

To avoid the crowd, I crossed the street in front of the Plot Thickens Book Store where I saw my Aunt Sandy browsing the stacks. I tapped on the window and waved. She gave me a thumbs up.

Keith and Randy were seated in Danny's Beer

Garden. I could see the tops of their heads over the stone wall Danny built to block it from the street and reroute the customers through the front door of the tavern.

Liz was not with them.

Keith wore a pair of faded Levi's, a white broadcloth shirt with the sleeves rolled up to the elbows and untucked, to hide his gun. His radio hung by a clip on the side of the front pocket.

Randy had on a pair of kaki chinos and a heather grey polo shirt. When he leaned forward, I noticed his weapon stuck in a holster at the small of his back. Both men had their hair combed. The sunset made Keith's hair shine even darker, if it were possible.

Randy's hair turned every color I saw in the sunset. As he turned his head toward me, the muted colors stayed where they were. The front of his unruly hair never behaved, no matter how much care he took.

Once I entered the outdoor beer garden, I ducked to lean under the umbrella stuck through a hole in the middle of the wrought iron table where they sat. I leaned both hands on it. I looked at Randy and then Keith. "Have either of you talked to Liz today?"

Randy blushed. "I did. I wanted to make sure she didn't change her mind about joining us."

I pulled out one of the red and white lawn chairs from under the table and perched on the edge of it.

"She isn't in her apartment and the lights were out on her floor when I passed the Moonstone Reflection. It's already after nine. It isn't like her to not check in if she's going to be late."

Both men stood at the same time. Keith turned to

Randy. "Did you drive?"

Randy shook his head *no*.

Keith said, "I walked too. By the time I sprint to the station or home to get a vehicle we could trace her steps by foot."

Randy threw a twenty-dollar bill on the table and we left.

Randy headed for the Moonstone Reflection to talk to the twenty-four-hour receptionist at the front desk.

Keith, Nutmeg and I went back to Liz's apartment.

Keith rapped gently on the door. "Liz, are you there?" He knocked louder and finally banged his fist on the door.

No answer or sound came from inside. In cop mode now, Keith pulled his Glock and turned toward me. "You're the landlady, open the door."

I liked to think I remained calm in all situations, yet my hands shook and I needed to put the code in more than once. I had a bad feeling about this.

"You and Nutmeg stay back until I make sure it's safe inside." A minute later he called for us to enter. "She isn't here. Nothing is out of place. It doesn't look as if she's been here all day. When did you last see her?"

I walked to the window and looked out as I told him. "The same time you did. Under the Hackberry tree outside the apartment building. She seemed relieved to find out she wasn't actually followed. She said she had a few loose ends to tie up at the office and she'd catch up with me later."

Keith came to my side. "Let's not get too excited

yet. Maybe she got called to a story. I'll get Randy on the phone and see what he found out."

Randy dashed into the room, out of breath and panting.

Nutmeg went from room to room with her nose in the air. She stopped and whined at the cabinet doors under the sink in the kitchen. Randy opened the door and looked into the trash can inside. My heart skipped a beat. My dog rarely led me in the wrong direction.

Randy picked a paper out of the trash can with a pair of tongs Keith found in a kitchen drawer.

Keith read over Randy's shoulder.

They looked at one another and I asked. "Come on guys, are you going to let me in on what it says?"

Randy looked at me and read the note again, out loud. *I don't want to hurt you. There are things about Mick you don't know. I'm willing to tell you the entire story. Meet me.*

I looked down and shook my head. "It doesn't say where he wanted to meet her. The lake is a big place with all the lake roads twisting and turning through the countryside. What shall we do?"

"Our best plan of action is to go back to the station and scour the security tapes of the Boardwalk," Keith said as he headed out the door. He didn't get very far when his radio came to life. He keyed it in and we all listened. "Chief. This is Officer Oliver Thurgood from the State Police. We found a body near Lake Road 27 and Route 13. I believe it's your murder victim from last week. Thought you might want to take over the case since he's yours."

Randy was in such a hurry to get out the door he

nearly tripped over Nutmeg who moved as fast as she could.

Keith stopped and leaned up against the trim on the door frame. "I'll call Amanda and have her scan the surveillance footage since noon today. Randy, you come with me. Ary, can you stay here in case she comes home?"

"Not hardly," I said, "I'll leave a few notes around town before I follow you. Liz is no idiot. If she gets free or is able, she will call."

Both men looked at me. No one said another word. Keith shook his head in exasperation and Randy followed him as he left the apartment.

CHAPTER THIRTEEN

I went to my apartment and changed into some clothes I could move better in. I put on a pair of faded jeans, a Moonstone Lake tee shirt and my Nike tennis shoes.

Nutmeg's food bowl was empty. I filled it, gave her fresh water and took a minute to catch my breath.

She didn't need an invitation. She gobbled down her dinner, drank some water and climbed on the couch beside me. I didn't move fast enough for her so she put her paw on my lap and gave out a half whine, half bark.

I dug my keys out of the desk drawer and headed toward our garage in back of the café.

Liz bought a Vespa 50cc scooter when Mick left for what we thought was prison.

The bike sat in front of my car with the cover on

it as it always did when it wasn't in use. I had one more clue. Where ever she went and however she got there she didn't go by scooter. For some reason, the knowledge made me feel worse than before.

Nutmeg and I arrived at the scene around ten-thirty.

The State Police, Highway Patrol, and Moonstone Lake Police Department all had cars around the area with lights flashing. Jess Morgan and his crew walked around and took pictures. Mick's body lie in a ditch barely off the roadway.

Keith knelt down next to the body. Jess pointed and talked. Keith nodded and listened. "Take several pictures of the money sticking out of his chest. I know it is a clue, but I don't know what the killer is trying to tell us."

Jess's camera flash went off several times in rapid succession. "Keith, remember what Liz told us what his last words were. I don't remember them verbatim, but the gest of it was the money was his and instead of protecting him, they kicked him to the curb.

"I'm sure it is symbolism, but it portrays the opposite of what he said. This looks more like he was killed because he had money that belonged to someone else."

Keith stood and moved toward Jess. "It's strange isn't it? Maybe the body will reveal more once we have an autopsy"

Randy and several of the other men searched the area. I could hardly believe a storm brewed in the southwest after the gorgeous sunset we had.

So much for *red sky in morning sailor take warning and red sky at night, sailor's delight.*

Nutmeg, who sat beside me, jumped to her feet and took off in a dead run toward the woods. I called but she didn't listen. I could hear her as she ran farther and farther into the woods that encircled the area.

I tried to calm myself down. *Nutmeg the wonder dog* I told myself time after time. If she were truly special, she could find her way back in the darkness. I might be afraid of the dark, but Nutmeg proved time and time again, it didn't bother her.

At least fifteen minutes passed before Nutmeg came bounding back with something in her mouth and laid it at Randy's feet. Randy looked at it for a long while and called for Jess and Keith. "Bring your equipment, we need to bag a piece of evidence. "

The two men jogged over and looked down. Jess took his camera he carried on a strap over his shoulder and began to snap pictures. When he wanted to see the other side of the object, he turned it over with a stick. He dusted the entire phone for finger prints and finally picked it up with what looked like long tweezers and slipped it into an evidence bag.

He held the bag in the air with two fingers. "Anyone recognize this?"

I answered. "Yes, it belongs to Liz Austin."

Keith looked at Nutmeg and asked. "Can you find the spot again, girl?"

Nutmeg barked twice and took off. Keith looked at me. "Is there any way you can get her to slow down? I couldn't run fast on my best day."

Jess picked up his equipment and Keith waited for him at the edge of the woods. Nutmeg ran out into the night, turned in circles, barked again and went back into the woods. I believed it to be the universal dog signal for follow me. I saw Rin Tin Tin and Lassie both do it over the years.

Most of the men followed Nutmeg into the woods and I ended up waiting with Mick Dudley's dead body. I looked down and saw the wad of money sticking out of the huge knife wound in this belly.

I didn't move until the EMTs transported him from the area.

I told them to go ahead and leave. "I'm a big girl," I said, "I'll be fine here."

The men weren't gone two full minutes when I heard something behind me, then beside me. It was drizzle ahead of the rain and storm close behind it.

I took a big breath of relief when I realized it as rain and not the boogie-man. I sat in my car, rolled up the windows and locked the doors.

I don't know how long it was before the men returned from the woods. Keith had a bag in his hand and Randy carried a forlorn look. I got out of the car. Nutmeg's coat smelled like wet dog. I removed a towel I kept in the trunk and began to dry her.

"What's that you have?" I asked of no one in particular.

"It's lipstick, scooter keys, and other odds and ends a woman keeps in her purse. No purse, no sign of Liz. The men decided to stop searching. The rain and us tramping around out there would destroy any clues there might be.

"I got a call from the coroner on call. He said we could come by and look at the body with him. Do you want to go along?"

"That's sweet Keith, but I think looking at the decaying and bug-ridden body once is all the fun I can handle." I looked at my phone for the time. "It's after three. I'm going home to bed. Feel free to wake me if there is any news on Liz, otherwise, I'm down for the count."

He gave me a sweet smile, helped me into my car and said, "Goodnight. I'll fill you in tomorrow morning."

Chapter Fourteen

I hated to wake Aunt Sandy in the middle of the night for the second time in a week, but I did. I correct my statement. I woke her at dawn. It took her forever to come to the door.

I'd made up my mind to go on to bed when Sandy slowly peeked out the door. Her jammies were bright blue with cats all over them. One reached in the air to bat a ball, another slept on his back with all four legs in the air and a third one sat ready to pounce. I put my hand over my eyes. "Don't those PJ's keep you up at night. They're pretty loud."

Sandy rubbed her eyes and said, "how can you have a sense of humor? The sun isn't even up."

She opened the door wider and motioned for me to come in. Nutmeg whined. She didn't want to go in and deal with the cats. She lay down by the side of the door with her head on her paws. The dog gave me a look that could mean nothing but, *don't make me.*

Aunt Sandy gave me the strangest look. "What is it?" She asked, "Is everything okay. Is it Emma?"

"No, no. it's about Liz Austin and Mick Dudley. Liz didn't show up at Danny's tonight and the State Police found Mick's body on a lake road. It's all so eerie.

"Nutmeg found a note in Liz's trash asking her to meet whoever wrote the note. He said he wanted to tell her all about Mick, the real story.

"I went to the site where the police found Mick. Nutmeg found Liz's phone in the surrounding woods. We also found some of the contents of her purse but no Liz. It began to rain and they had to call off the search."

At this point she grabbed my hand and said, "You need to come in and sit down."

I looked back over my shoulder and invited Nutmeg to come in and join us. She answered by stretching out and turning on her side and added a lazy yawn to reinforce her answer.

"I saw Liz and a young man about seven o'clock. They strolled down the Boardwalk. He even held her arm. I smiled at them and said *hi*. They both smiled back."

I fell into the chair behind me. "It had to be the man who wrote the note."

I took my phone from my pocket and called Keith. It was a little after six. He came to Sandy's apartment within a couple of minutes. "Can you tell me about the man you saw with Liz?

"Sure, he wasn't someone you would soon forget.

He looked a lot like Mick; same build, weight and hair color. He had the ever-popular two-day growth."

Keith took notes, "How was he dressed?"

"It's the one thing I noticed about him that was off. He wore a tight-fitting gray polo shirt, one with the horse on the front. His upper arms were muscled and tanned. He wore white cargo shorts that hugged his legs showing off the muscles beneath them also. I'd say he either had a job that required muscle or he worked out a lot. The odd thing was his shoes. He had on black dress shoes and black socks."

"Where did you see them?"

"They were walking toward here."

"Sandy, can you show me how he held her arm?"

Keith stood next to her. She bent his arm and held him by placing her hand firmly on his elbow.

Keith looked from one of us to the other. "I don't believe it was a friendly walk. All he had to do was squeeze her elbow and the pain would keep her in line. Is that the only time you saw them?"

"Later I saw Liz hurry down the alley between the Christmas store and the flower shop. I waved at her when she passed but she didn't wave or look my way. "

Keith tapped his pen against the pad he wrote on. "Are you sure it was Liz?"

"Positive."

"What time was that?"

Sandy leaned forward. "It was nearly dark.

"Sandra, I know you have a restaurant to run, but can you find time to meet with a police sketch artist?"

"Sure, we have enough help. When and where?"

"We don't have an artist here. I'll have to get one

from Stanfield. I'm sure it will be later today." He turned his attention to me. "Are you going back out to the crime scene with me?"

"I need to shower and to make sure everyone came to work and breakfast is on track. I'll try to drive out in a couple of hours." I grinned. Are you sure I won't get in the way?"

By now we were standing outside my door. "Do you have any ideas?"

"I don't have any ideas per say, but Mick had to have had some parents when he grew up. Do you know anything about them?

"Rumor had it his parents were older. Maybe in their late sixties. They would be past eighty now if they are alive and still live in Moonstone Lake. I don't know much about them. I've never thought about it. I guess I was too self-absorbed in grade school and high school to notice. He was older and rarely in the same place as I was. I can honestly say if I ever met or saw his folks, it is gone from my memory."

He leaned down and touched his lips lightly on mine. "I'll see you later."

And he was gone.

I leaned against my door for a long minute. His closeness lit a spark in me. I pulled myself out of my stupor and made myself move on with my day.

Nutmeg danced around to go for our run. I didn't have the energy. "Can you go by yourself? I'll get you something special from the kitchen when you get back."

It took longer to dress than I thought it would, I needed to wear something nice enough for the café and casual enough to wear if I decided to help search the woods with Keith and the others. I decided on long navy-blue shorts with no pockets, a pink button up shirt with long sleeves I rolled up to the elbow. My thought was I could roll them down later so as not to scratch my arms if I went to the woods. My Nike's were still wet from the night before and I pulled out my oxblood colored leather loafers and slipped them on.

CHAPTER FIFTEEN

I needn't have worried about the café. Benny had everything running smoothly. The dining room filled up quickly. After a couple of hours, I left the café in his capable hands and skipped out. If a problem should arise, Aunt Sandy would be around and she could do everything I could do.

I needed to get Nutmeg to the groomer. We missed her last two appointments and with the rain the night before, she gave off an eye squinting, nose crinkling smell. The only thing worse than a wet smelly dog was a dry smelly dog who sleeps with you.

She would not be happy when I left her with the groomer and rushed off to visit the crime scene and catch up on any new developments.

Pawsitively Devine Groomers didn't have anyone

waiting. Shelly, the owner, said if I could wait forty-five-minutes I could take my dog with me.

I went to Lakeside Discount groceries next door and picked out snacks for whoever might be a searcher in the woods. I put two cases of water in my back seat.

A man I saw caused me to make a double take.

Six feet tall, black curly hair, neat two-day stubble and Big Screen good looks. He didn't have a grocery cart. He held everything in his rock-solid arms. I saw Cheese Its, water, and Liz's favorite, HoHo's. I was sure I found the kidnapper.

It made me feel better to know she might not be in the woods hurt. I got a sudden chill and decided this might be worse.

The stranger checked out, paid with cash and left. My car was in the groomer's parking lot. If I went to get it, I wouldn't know what he drove. If I followed him on foot and he drove off, well, I was sunk one way or another.

I reached for my phone and realized I didn't have it. I picked out pants with no pockets. My phone lay on the dresser in my apartment.

My only choice was to follow him. The one thing about tourist towns is there are people milling around everywhere. I easily blended into the crowd.

I followed him down the street where he turned left and walked another two blocks, and made a right.

When he made the second turn I was forced to stop. He and I would have been the only people on the block.

It was a residential neighborhood where locals lived. I stood on the porch of a stained-glass shop and peaked around the corner of the building. A few minutes later he drove by in a Dodge Ram dually truck with Indiana plates XAD 126.

I chastised myself for not having a car or a phone. I ran back to Pawsitively. There sat Nutmeg clean, toenails cut and a pink bandana around her neck. She hated the bandana part and I took it off as soon as we were out of Shelly's sight.

I hurried to the car and went the same direction as the big truck. I knew I didn't have much of a chance to find him but I went anyway. Three miles outside of town, just off the Interstate I spotted him. His truck sat in a convenience store parking lot at the gas pump closest to the road. I pulled up to the pump in front of him and on the other side. I rolled down the window for Nutmeg and began to put gas in the car. My face turned scarlet when I realized again, I had no money.

I moved the car to a parking space in front of the store and went in. I knew I didn't have to have money to dial 911.

The young lady working behind the counter, a pretty brunette about twenty, smiled at me when I walked in. Her name tag read Bambi S. She had curly brown hair, a vivid red top that barely came to her navel and white shorts that hardly covered all they should. I tried not to stare.

I told myself I was young once. Get a grip; I never dressed like that. If Mom didn't send me back to change clothes; Aunt Sandy surely would have. She stopped chewing her gum long enough to let me use the phone.

"911," a voice I didn't recognize answered.

"What is your emergency?"

"I am following a truck outside Moonstone Lake on Highway 13. I need for someone to call Chief Keith Wesley of the Moonstone Lake Police and give him the plate number.

"Miss, I know this sounds odd but if you tell him it is Arizona he will understand.

"We are driving toward the Lake Loop East. The truck is a late model Dodge Ram four door dually, Indiana license plate XAD126."

I didn't know whether to wait for Keith to call me back or to follow the truck. At the last minute I chose to follow the truck. During the day most people were on the water. There was no traffic. I had to hang back, sometimes a half mile around a curve so he wouldn't see me.

The driver turned down an unmarked road. It was too overgrown with weeds and untrimmed shrubs for me to see what sat at the end of the lane. I drove a quarter of a mile past the road and parked the car. "Nutmeg," I said, "I need to see if Liz is with the man in the truck. I know you will want to go and I pray you understand what I'm telling you. We can't make any noise. No growling or barking. Do you understand?"

The dog put her two front paws on my arm. I had to take it as a *yes* because I had nothing else.

I got out of the car and went around to free Nutmeg. I judged it to be about two o'clock in the afternoon. We would have plenty of daylight.

There was a foot path to the west of the main road, or drive. The Dodge truck sat outside next to an old Chevy truck painted red patches of primer showing and a new shiny black Impala with the vanity plate *Gld Mine*. I stayed behind a large maple tree and stood to listen. Nutmeg took my shorts in her mouth and gently pulled me toward the back of the house.

I followed her. I could hear voices inside. We ducted under an open window and listened.

"What did you do with the girl?" An older sounding gruff voice said.

Another voice, much younger sounding answered. "I left her in the National Forest where someone is bound to find her. I swear, she doesn't know anything. She swore to me Mick didn't have any money.

"I explained to her about where the money came from and she said again, if Mick had money, he kept it from her. She's a nice lady and I didn't give her enough information to hurt us."

A woman with a soft voice spoke up, "after all these years of running the perfect operation, some know nothing kid from Podunk Ville sees an article and realizes he is the heir to millions of dollars. When you wanted to hide him with the Dudley's in Moonstone Lake, I knew you were wrong. I should have had you shoot him back then. We wouldn't be any worse off than we are now."

The older man laughed an evil laugh; then a solitary gunshot echoed through the cabin.

Involuntarily I let an *aah* escape my mouth.

It turned deadly quiet in the house. I don't think anyone even breathed. Nutmeg ran to the trunk of an oak and acted like she had something treed. An older man came out. I got a good look at her before he turned to go back into the house.

He had to have been in his seventies. The only hair I saw ringed the back of his neck and ran above his ears. He wore dark gray dress pants with a short sleeve white dress shirt, tucked in.

His shoes were black and looked new or newly shined. He was trim and fit. He looked like every other business man I'd ever met.

"It's only a dog after a squirrel. Help me bury this traitor."

A woman answered. "You killed him. You bury him. Amos, you just made your biggest mistake. We've been embezzling money from the rich for almost twenty-five years and you intend to let one man ruin it all?

"Now, when the cops find Justin, they will show the girl a picture and they will know it was him who kidnapped her. It won't be long until they trace everything back to you and me. And we still don't have what we need from Dudley. It was just another unnecessary death. What do you intend to do next?"

"As soon as I find the papers, or key or whatever that fool Mick Dudley hid that prove he is the heir to the money I'm going someplace far away. I haven't spent much of the money we have skimmed over the years. All but traveling money is off shore. I want the money Mick stashed because it has been in the same place for over twenty-years. We can spend the cash and no one will trace it.

"I've always wanted to live in France. I have my new name all picked out. The passport and the other documents are ready, once we find the money, we are free and clear."

"You old fool, it isn't that simple, the lady said,

what about Daniel, he has done the legal work. He'd be easy to trace. Do you think it is fair to leave? He'll end up holding the bag."

"Martha, I have bigger fish to fry. Send him a message that it's over. It'll give him a bit of a head start. Wish him luck. He has to have more than ten million dollars stashed. He will be fine.

"I guess this is the last time we will see one another. You forget my name and I'll forget yours."

"Amos, you haven't said where you are going."

"Just suffice to say, wherever it is, I will be on the golf course every day. There is still time for us to make arrangements to be together."

"You're kidding right? I don't want to hurt your feelings, but I intend to forget everyone I know around Chicago, especially you!"

I heard the chair scrape on the wooden floor. I saw the top of her head and platinum hair as she got out of her chair. "By the way Amos, how long are we going to try to find the papers?"

"I've been thinking about it. If we don't have it in a month, I intend to burn Moonstone Lake and everything in it to the ground. No one will find it then."

I could see her shake her head at him. "We know the money is in bearer bonds in a safe deposit box in Chicago. Why not just go in and take it?"

Nutmeg and I ran as fast as we could to the car and headed toward the service station. I called Keith from.

As I drove toward it, I saw flashing lights. Keith's cruiser and a Highway Patrol car sat in front of the door. The officers were in the store talking to the clerk.

When Keith saw me through the window, he ran to me and wrapped me in his arms. After a long minute he pushed me back to look me in the eyes, I never saw such a look on his face. I didn't think he would let me go. When he did his eyes flashed in rage. "Do you remember when you found the body in Moonstone Lake and you couldn't call the police because you didn't have your phone?" He loosened his grip on me. "I thought you learned your lesson. Am I going to have to put a GPS tracker on Nutmeg?"

I smiled, he didn't.

Nutmeg pushed her way between us and Keith settled down a bit.

CHAPTER SIXTEEN

All Keith had to say was, "Well?"

I told him about the cabin and the three people who spoke. I told them I heard but did not see the man called Amos shoot the man I was sure kidnapped Liz.

Keith took his attention off me and asked Johnson if he thought they needed back up to check out the cabin. Johnson said yes and got on his radio to arrange it. Moonstone Lake's police force had Amanda, Randy, Keith and two part time cops who patrolled at night. One stayed on the south side of the lake and one on the north. Not much happened after dark at the lake. Most of the folks spent their days on the water, came in town to shop or eat and were in bed or sitting in front of a bonfire by eleven o'clock.

"What about Liz?" I asked, "are you going to send

some men to the National Forest?"

"Ary, you aren't thinking straight. The forest is over four million acres. Once we round these people up, we will find out where she is.

"What else do you remember?"

"He paid cash for the gas, bought a Coke, and a couple of snacks. We followed him to the cabin and I told you everything about what happened there. The strange thing is I first spotted him at Lakeside Grocery and he bought snacks there also."

"Do you realize what danger you put yourself in? One sneeze or if you tripped over a twig you might have been shot too. I swear Arizona; If you don't care what happens to you, think about those of us around you."

"But Keith, did you follow all I told you; their first names, they were from the Chicago area. The thefts have been going on for twenty-five years and now we have enough to find them and stop the entire operation. I forgot one thing they said, if they don't find Mick's safe deposit key in the next month. We will see that all of Moonstone Lake burns to the ground. He's a horrible man, Keith."

I looked out the front window. Nutmeg had her nose to the pane; the saddest look on her face and an empty cigarette pack in her mouth.

The three of us went outside to where Nutmeg wagged her tail and ran around in happy circles. "What do you have?" I said and tried to take the paper out of her mouth. She growled, not a mad growl but one I knew meant, *this is mine, don't take it.*

She pranced over to Keith, looked up at him and

dropped the pack on his foot. We could all see it had a note between the cellophane and the paper.

Keith went to his car and came back with rubber gloves. He pulled them on and picked up the cigarette package. Slowly and carefully he slipped the card out and held it up. One side had Liz Austin's address and on the other side a phone number.

Keith wrote the number down in the small notebook he carried in his front pocket.

Johnson held up an evidence bag and Keith slipped the card inside along with the cigarette package. The officer put it in his front pocket and patted it. "I'll get this to the lab if you don't need me anymore. We have three cars on the way and Catoosa County is sending two,

The two men shook hands. Keith turned to me. "How did you have Nutmeg groomed without money, and how did you manage to leave the house with nothing?"

I didn't know why I felt like a small child being reprimanded by her favorite uncle, but I did. "I have no reason you would think good enough to justify leaving everything at home. To answer one of your questions, I have an account at the groomers."

We drifted toward his car. He opened his door yet didn't get in. "Ary, I know Moonstone Lake is one of the safest places in the country. I've been here less than a year and this is the second murder. Everyone, even the people in your town can lose their tempers. The two people who were killed didn't live here. One was here for a wedding and Mick; well I don't know why Mick was here. After what you told me, I think we had better put our full time and effort into finding whatever it is that is so important to these people.

"I don't profess to be a genius, but I know buying and selling commodities and trading stock can be a cash business. If they have done this for over twenty-five years, there are many more Mick's out there. They just may not know they have been cheated.

Mick couldn't have been more than five or six when they stashed him in Moonstone Lake. I wonder why he didn't say anything to the people he lived with. He had to feel comfortable or he would have told someone over the years."

He stopped talking and took my hand. He obviously wasn't done talking to me about what he considered my disregard for my own safety.

"Think about this. There are six or seven thousand people you don't know in this town at any given time. I know you are a grown woman, but please listen to me about this. Had you run out of gas on the road you would have been out there on your own. No money, no phone, believe me, it's difficult to get someone to stop and if they don't want to help you, there is nothing you can do."

Before we had time to say anything else, police cars came into the parking lot from all directions. By the time they all stopped there was a circle of flashing lights.

The man who seemed to be in charge marched up with a map in his hand. I know you have your hands full Chief Wesley. Show us where the cabin is and we will take care of it. Of course, because of the location I'll have to hold the perps in custody at the facility until we straighten this out."

I looked back and forth at them. They were

playing king of the hill and Keith let the other guy win.

Keith's phone rang. "Yes, this is Keith Wesley. Yes; I'm Chief of Police in Moonstone Lake. Yes, I know a Liz Austin. Where? When? Is she okay? Thanks Captain Ogden. We will be there as soon as we can."

He hung up and began to pace.

"What? I asked him, "What happened?"

"That was the Captain of Park Rangers from the Southern section of Truman National Forest. A woman was found on one of the top trails at Granite Pass. He didn't have much information about her. They said it was Liz Austin. They are getting ready to bring her down. She's off the path but found by some hikers. "Can you go to the search and tell Randy about this phone call? If I tell him on my radio, he will take off like a bat and I want him to get there in one piece.

"First, I need you to show or tell these officers about the cabin, the cars you saw there and all of the license plate numbers. Can you do that?" He saw the fire in my eyes and changed *can you do that* to *will you do it*?"

"Sure, I'll do anything I can to help."

"Thanks, I'll be at FR-11-S at the ranger station. They are posting someone at the gate who will have directions to where Liz is. Please go home, get your phone and maybe get a purse or jeans with pockets and I'll see you there later."

He pulled out of the parking lot, turned on his siren and sped out of sight.

CHAPTER SEVENTEEN

I told the police how to get to the cabin. The man in charge gave me a pencil and piece of paper so I could draw a sketch of the road, the path and where the trucks were parked, the car, and about the open back window. I told them about the man they shot up there. I said I didn't know what they did with his body. It all took less than five minutes and I headed back toward Moonstone Lake.

Nutmeg sat as far away from me as she could and looked out the window on the passenger side. It wasn't like her but I knew what bothered her. "It's okay, Nutmeg. Keith didn't mean not to thank you. He has a lot on his mind. Don't be too upset with him.'

She whined, turned toward me and lay down with her head on my leg. I patted her. Had anyone else been with me in the car, they would have thought me crazy. People love praise, dogs thrive on it.

I didn't want to be the one to tell Randy about Liz. It would be different if I knew her condition. Keith thought it might temper the shock, I didn't.

As I pulled up, I saw Amanda, Randy, and a State Trooper against a police car. They looked like death warmed over. Randy had dark circles under his eyes, his uniform had a thousand wrinkles and his boots were covered with mud. Amanda and the officer looked slightly better.

"Hi Randy, Amanda, Officer," He held his hand out to me.

"I'm, John, John Allen."

"It's nice to meet you John. Keith sent me to give you some news he didn't want to send   over the airways." They all looked at me with hollow eyes. "Liz has been found in the National Forest."

Randy headed for his cruiser. "Wait," I shouted. "This is why Keith sent me instead of using the radio. He doesn't want you to take off in a hurry and get hurt. Take a deep breath."

Randy turned toward me, stopped and put both his hands on his hips. The look he gave me is not one you'd give to a friend. "Are you saying Keith doesn't want me there?"

"I'm not saying that at all. He knows you are tired and worried. I had the feeling he only wanted to have you take a breath and calm yourself a little before you go."

Amanda went to his side and put her hand on his arm. "She's right, Randy. You're tired and out of sorts. You smell like you have been camping for a week. If we get there in an hour or an hour and a half, nothing is going to change.

"I'll follow you back to town. We can shower put on clean clothes and meet at the station as soon as we are cleaned up. Say in a half an hour."

He looked at me and I shook my head yes as did Amanda.

The three of us and Nutmeg drove back to Moonstone Lake. The patrolman called his supervisor and told him the news. He waved as he headed off in the opposite direction.

I stopped at the apartment, put on a pair of jeans with big pockets and a bright red scoop neck tee. My phone stuck out of my back pocket and I tucked a few dollars in the front. Five minutes later I stood in the front foyer of the restaurant with Aunt Sandy. "Howdy stranger, how's the investigation going?"

As quickly as I could I gave her the highlights. Nutmeg and I went outside and waited for someone to pick us up. Randy skidded up to the curb and said, 'Hop in, any word from Keith?"

My face reddened. It hadn't occurred to me to check for missed calls. I pulled my phone out of my pocket and checked. "Not a word." I said.

The Truman National Forest covered most of the Ozark Highlands. Some of its million's acres included campgrounds and hiking trails. Other sections were extreme terrain with sink holes, black bears and mountain lions. The forest included the St. Francois Mountains as well as dry rocky glades and prairie land.

If a hiker fell or had a medical emergency and ended up off the trail, it could be years before he was found. That someone found Liz was a blessing. Truman Forest didn't fall inside the city limits of Moonstone Lake or even in Catoosa County.

Though the guys had no authority in the forest, we knew those in charge would treat them as if they did.

The drive took over an hour. Randy tried to make up for the time we took to clean up by driving too fast. He'd changed into blue chinos, a polo shirt with the Moonstone Lake Police logo on the left chest and his name in small letters below it. He wore his utility belt with his gun, pepper spray, extra ammo and his badge. His boots were spit shined.

Amanda had on the exact same outfit, somehow it looked feminine on her slim athletic body. Her hair hung in a loose ponytail down her back.

Although his usual even temperament and quick smile were hidden, Randy's appeal was ever present.

Amanda wanted to take her own cruiser. She didn't intend to stay. Since Liz went missing the police department was short staffed and the Sheriff's Department of Catoosa County had taken up the slack.

We pulled into the parking lot. A ranger walked up to the car and directed us to the area where we would find Keith. We had no problem finding it with an ambulance, a search and rescue truck all with lights flashing. Four para-medics carried a stretcher down the path.

I stood on my tip toes to see if the face of the victim had a sheet over it. It did not. I let out an audible sigh of relief.

As soon as Randy saw what I saw he ran toward her. Keith, the ranger captain and the medics walked alongside the transport stretcher until the men pulled the legs out and let it stand alone. "Liz?" Randy said as he stepped up and took her hand. "Are you okay?"

She smiled and squeezed his hand. "As well as can be expected for someone who slept behind a rock with no pillow or blanket." She tried to smile. Her lips were chapped and although the EMT's had covered her with several blankets, she shook from the cold. Her hair clung to her bruised face.

"Are you hurt?"

Keith gently pushed Randy back a step and turned him so they were face to face. "I know you are curious, we all are. An emergency doctor came with them. They are taking her back to the hospital. Once she is warm and fed, we can talk to her. Doctor said she is most likely okay but he wants to be sure. Hypothermia is a for sure. She says the man didn't lay a hand on her. I consider her extremely lucky."

Keith put a hand on each hip. In an uncharacteristic tone he said, "We'll all go over and be there when we get the okay to question her. You can wait a little longer, can't you Deputy Malone?"

Randy said nothing, He stepped to the side and let the men put Liz in the ambulance and take her away. They didn't use a siren which I considered a good sign,

Amanda came up to where we all stood. "Chief, I know you're busy but may I speak to you a second?"

"Sure." They stepped away from the group.

Amanda left shortly thereafter.

Randy and I stayed at the park and listened to Keith question the two young hikers who found our friend.

The young couple tried to hike in a different spot every weekend. They picked the Granite Pass path because the outside temperature soared over ninety degrees and the trail was known to be one of the shadiest.

The couple hiked to the top of the glacier pack, had a picnic lunch and started back down. Out of nowhere, a storm came up and a downpour soaked them.

Dana and Dennis were boyfriend, girlfriend. They were dressed in conventional gear with cargo shorts, long sleeve shirts and hiking boots. They wore bucket hats and Dennis had a huge hunting knife attached to his belt.

Dana said the path down the side of the mountain had ruts and water due to the rain. She slipped and slid off the path behind a huge bolder.

Dennis walked over to help his sweetheart up and they spotted a woman unconscious behind a tree. The woman didn't move when she shook her. From the bruise on her face they assumed she hit her head on the rock. Tracks and marks on the ground told them she most likely scooted under the tree during the storm.

Dana took Liz's pulse and said it was strong but slow. Dennis had a silver emergency blanket in his backpack. They covered Liz.

Cell phones were useless so far up the mountain. Dana stayed with Liz and Dennis went to fetch a ranger.

Liz stirred and Dana gave her sips of water and rubbed her arms to help with circulation. Other than those two gestures, she didn't know what else to do.

The ranger on duty, an older man who looked as if he would never make it to the top of a hill; much less a mountain path, called 911 and Captain Ogden.

The rangers had done many a rescue in the forest but when they learned her name, they decided not to move her until the authorities arrived.

Randy, who took down the couple's statements, thanked them over and over again. He took down their personal information and let them go.

Once loose ends were tied up at Granite Pass, Keith and Randy decided it would be best if Randy headed to the hospital to keep an eye on Liz. Keith would take me back to Moonstone Lake with him.

The first ten minutes of the ride home were quiet. The only sound in the car was Nutmeg's breathing as she snoozed on the back seat.

Finally, Keith said, "it's been a long couple of days and brings up more unknowns than we had before. Poor Liz had to have been terrified."

I turned toward him. "I wonder if the man I followed is the same man who left Liz on the mountain."

I don't profess to be a great reader of people but it didn't take one to know Keith didn't want to talk. After another long pause I leaned my head on the window, closed my eyes and rested. I went to sleep and didn't wake up until we were stopped in front of the restaurant.

Keith gently laid his arm on my shoulder. "Mind if I don't walk up with you?" He glanced at his watch. "I need to make some phone calls before it gets any later."

I opened my door. "No, that's fine. It isn't dark

yet and I have my four-legged bodyguard with me."

He smiled, but his eyes betrayed him. I could see the fatigue and worry in them. "I'm sorry Ari. This case has me stuck. Besides it involves two of my favorite people. The questions keep piling upon one another. You said the people in the cabin gave you the impression Mick uncovered an embezzlement group. What it has to do with his inheritance, or cash or whatever is beyond me.

"Is the fact he was killed outside Liz's apartment meaningful or a fluke? Why did someone kidnap Liz and leave her without food, water or even a jacket half way up a mountain trail in the National Forest? And if the man at the cabin who was killed is the same one who took Liz, why did they kill him. And the one that bugs me the most, what is the deal about Mick's body? Why take Mick Dudley's body and dump it again later. If the money sticking out of the wound is some sort of clue, it was lost on all of us. It would only be relative if we knew about the money in the first place. If someone needed proof of death, why not just take a picture?

"I'll talk to you tomorrow. Thanks for being such a sport and hanging in so long." He turned to Nutmeg. "Thanks lady, you found a clue at the filling station, and sat quietly when you needed to. You're a great dog."

Nutmeg stood next to the car door on my side and wagged her tail. I leaned over to pat Keith's arm and said, "Try to get some sleep. Liz is safe in the hospital; Randy is with her. The man in the truck is either dead or long gone and all the same questions will be here tomorrow when you are rested."

As I strolled up the walk to the café. I turned and waved at him. He waved back, made a U-turn and headed toward the police station.

CHAPTER EIGHTEEN

The café' hummed with voices and laughter. What a difference between the moods inside and outside of the building. I stood by the door to the dining room for a moment and took it all in. On my way back to the kitchen to visit with Louis; I stopped by a few tables and chatted with the diners.

Lewis sat at his desk with an order pad making notes. I never walked into his space that he wasn't busy. A couple of minutes later he looked up. "Hi Arizona, I heard on the news they found Liz unhurt on a mountain path several hours from here. I'm glad she is okay. The entire ordeal is bizarre. Hope they find Mick Dudley's killer soon. What can I do for you? Want to add something to tomorrow's order?"

"No, but you might need too. With Mom's problem, Mick's murder and now Liz's kidnapping;

Mom's birthday slips in and out of my mind. Feel like planning a party while we are here together?"

He grinned at me and moved to the kitchen side of the counter. "You look exhausted. Let me fix you something to eat while we talk. What are you hungry for?"

I hadn't thought about food but the mere mention of it made my stomach clinch. "I'll eat the special."

He patted my hand. "Not tonight." He called to Jason, our newest line cook, and said, "Would you please make Ary a grilled cheese sandwich on rye bread, a salad with ranch dressing on the side, a cup of tomato basil soup, a chocolate shake and a large serving of cheese cake with raspberries. She will eat it here."

I laughed. Louis came to work at Moonstone Café and Sunday Buffet when I was in the sixth grade. It was that time in my life when I had spindly legs, unruly hair and little self- esteem.

Mom stayed busy from morning to night. Aunt Sandy and Louis were more like my parents than Emma. I ate most of my meals on the very stool I occupied now. Most of the time, even back then, Louis took time to sit and keep me company. He said children should not eat alone.

On busy days when he didn't have time to spend with me, Aunt Sandra appeared out of nowhere and took over.

Louis had opportunity after opportunity to move up the line to bigger and better jobs. For years he owned and operated Chez Louie in Manhattan and had two Michelin stars.

He would never say what made him sell out and

bring his young family to the Midwest. His reputation followed him. Foodies stopped by to eat at Moonstone Café when they were in our area.

"The party is not a problem. I knew it was around the corner. I have the menu planned." He tipped his head back and chuckled. "She has had the same food on her birthday for the past twenty years. We'll have chili dogs, chips, ice tea and my famous caramel cupcakes with caramel icing."

"I always wondered why she chose chili dogs when she could have anything she wanted."

"Your mother is a generous woman. She wants to offer her birthday food to everyone and anyone who comes in the restaurant on her birthday."

I guess I never thought about it. The dining room with the overflow open, seated one hundred and fifty-two. "Her birthday is on Friday, so want to move it to Sunday as usual?"

We stopped our discussion when my dinner arrived. I ate in a peaceful silence with Louis who I loved like a favorite uncle.

Before I left, he asked, "I looked it up yesterday, we cooked 550 hotdogs, served 100 pounds of chips and sixty gallons of ice tea. I'll get someone on the cupcakes early and we'll freeze them. It worked well last year when we baked 60 dozen. Sound good to you?"

"You're an amazing man, Chef Louis. Thanks."

Louis came to my side of the counter and gave me a light hug. "You know, Arizona, this place runs fine without you and Sandy and your mother. You might want to think about taking a few more days off when you need them."

I couldn't help but laugh. "You know what Mother says…"

We said it together. *The reason the restaurant runs so well when we are gone is because it is so rare.*

We spent a few minutes talking about his grandchildren and wife.

CHAPTER NINETEEN

Keith walked up behind me. I glanced at him and then at my phone to check the time. "Need some breakfast? You're cutting it close. We switch to lunch in twenty minutes."

He plopped down on the nearest chair. "I'm too tired to eat. I thought I would drop by and see if I could get some sandwiches to take back to the National Forest. I swear we have been up and down the mountain three times and talked to everyone. Randy is sure we will find a clue as to who the bad guys are if we look long enough. If he came upon a bear, he would try to question him too."

He laid his head in his lap and didn't bother to look up again. I called Jamie over to the table to order him a cheeseburger and a cup of black coffee.

It was a good two minutes before he looked at me

again. "I'm sorry. I haven't had much sleep for three days and the fresh air up on the mountain is intoxicating.

Jamie put the coffee on the table and returned later with a burger with all the trimmings.

Twice while Keith sat there trying to eat his sandwich, his eyes closed and his head nearly hit the table.

I sat beside him and put my hand on his arm. I startled him and he jumped. "Listen, Keith, you are too sleepy to drive anywhere. Go upstairs and take a nap. My apartment is cool and relaxing. Just don't say one word about how messy it is."

"What about the sandwiches for the crew?"

"I'm convinced you wouldn't make it there without falling asleep. They will be alright. You aren't the only person taking them food. Captain Woods from the Highway Patrol came in about six and picked up food he said was for the searchers.

We are supposed to meet at Liz's tonight. This will give you another few hours to plant yourself in one place."

He stood, turned toward the doors, but reached back for his hamburger on his way.

"Want to know about Liz before I go?'

I nodded yes.

"She's fine. The description of the man you followed and the one who took Liz are one in the same. He told Liz to call him Justin. We found him in a shallow grave at the cabin.

. Liz said Mick had a birthmark of the same three dots on his neck below his left ear and a little forward. She said the man who kidnapped her had the exact same birthmark.

"Maybe they were related. It is not unusual for people in the same gene pool to have the same birthmark. They used him to get to Mick and then disposed of him. I have a hunch they are still in business. That would be nearly thirty years, or maybe more. Didn't you say Amos said twenty-five years. If Mick had millions, how much do you think they stole over the last decades?

"Mick must have been the key to catching them. He hid something they are still afraid of. We need to find it before they destroy Moonstone Lake to protect themselves.

"We put a BOLO out on the truck, which was gone when the troopers arrived. Earlier this morning a fisherman went to open his cabin on Kenoma Lake in Barton County. He spotted the top of the truck in the lake and called authorities. I believe they are making plans to pull it out now.

"The old truck you described was still parked in the lane but the Impala was gone. There was more than one way out and they took it.

"I'm on my way to talk to the coroner to see what else I can find out about Mick and the other dead man.

"One more thing, the plates on the Dodge Ram were stolen a few weeks ago from a Range Rover in Columbus, Indiana.

"I have a favor which is above and beyond the duties of a friend."

I slipped into the booth and sat across from him. "What do you need?"

"Can you go to Stanfield Memorial and pick Liz

up?"

"Does it matter when?"

"Sometime after one, they begin discharging patients at noon. She is in room 410. Of course, MSPD will reimburse you. Just write down your mileage."

"Where is everyone?" I asked.

"Randy is in the forest. Amanda is with Mick's body in Stanfield. Marshall and Dallas are here in town. If you don't want to go or don't have time, just tell me, I'll figure something out."

"No, I can go. Don't worry about it."

"The other reason I'd like you to go is because Liz is pretty closed up about what the man said and did. The most I can get out of her is he picked her up from the Boardwalk, after lunch. He drove her to Yellville to a place called the Restaurant Across the Creek. He took a road behind the building and drove to a cabin a few minutes down a dirt road.

"There was a small garage there. It had two chairs inside. He sat her down and told her he didn't want to see her get hurt. He said one way or another Mick would have ended up murdered. He said his name was Justin and he came to save Mick but it was too late when he got there. He said he was Mick's older brother and he thought if he talked to Mick, he could save him.

"He told her Mick's only crime was to be born into a family that chose the wrong people to manage their money. He told her Mick had information on where his money was.

"Before he told her anything else or she could ask questions, they heard voices. He grabbed her and they ran to the truck. She said he never uttered a word after that and took her to Granite Pass by the service roads posted *no admittance*.

"He let her out and told her *to save lives she needed to find the information and turn it over to the authorities. I'm not positive what it is. They keep talking about a safe deposit box. Maybe it is a key, or maybe he cashed it in for something of the same value.*

"Her knee is all cut and bruised as is her face. Liz asked me if I could imagine how many unidentifiable sounds there are in the dark on the mountain."

"She said he was articulate, clean, well dressed and soft spoken. Liz asked him about the birthmark and he laughed, and told her there were five brothers. They all had the birthmark. He said he was Mick's last hope. They killed him. Actually, they killed all five boys; over money.

Ann brought a bag of food to the table. Keith took it and left.

What could it be? Liz had to have something she didn't know she had. Justin was going to help her find it.; they killed him.

CHAPTER TWENTY

I didn't turn on the radio on my drive to Stanfield. I took the time to go over all I knew about the murders, which wasn't much.

Once I retrieved Liz and got her settled at home, we needed to get organized and find the secret. One important enough to kill Mick and now his brother, Justin.

Then I remembered what I heard in the cabin. Amos said, "I thought the birthmark would be enough to prove who you were. I didn't think you would be dumb enough to meet him without a plan. I also didn't think Mick could outsmart you."

Without another word, he called Justin a traitor and shot him. That was a clue. Justin said he recognized Mick because of the tattoo but in this big wide world, how did he know to look for Mick in

Moonstone Lake? This had everything to do with the coverup between Mick and the authorities. They'd sent him to Indiana, but why?

In the back of my mind I had a nagging thought the mystery began when Mick was a small child. They gave him some papers to ensure his future and sent him off to the lake. Now I think it was for his own safety.

An orderly stood behind Liz Austin. I saw her turn to him and point me out, He smiled and pushed Liz to the door. She gingerly stood and moved toward the car. She wore a green hospital scrub top and pants to match. She had nothing else with her when they brought her down from the mountain.

She turned to the young man with the chair and thanked him. When she turned to me, she said cheerfully, "You're a sight for sore eyes. Thanks for rescuing me."

I smiled at her. "You had us all worried. I thought about you and me on the way here. Two little girls jumping and playing from daylight to dark, without a care in the world. Now we need to find a killer before he strikes out at someone else."

I drove through a Dairy Queen and bought milkshakes and chicken strips with gravy. They were a favorite of mine. I considered gravy a comfort food. We munched and settled in for the drive back to Moonstone Lake. A three-and-a-half-hour drive became a two-hour drive if you drove through Truman National Forest. I loved the drive through the forest. No matter what time of day you made the trip, deer, rabbits, squirrels, and an occasional turtle crossed your path. Very few other cars or people were to be seen.

"You know, Ari? I had a great childhood. Mom and Dad left the world too soon but I have never been so alone as I feel now. Had I listened to one person, I wouldn't have been with Mick and none of this would have happened." Tears rolled down her cheeks.

"We all make mistakes and look back to see what might have been. Once I realized what *hindsight is 20-20* meant and understood it; I try to move on and not second guess myself."

"Remember, you did what was right for you with the information you had at the time. Don't beat yourself up. Besides, you are not all alone. What about Randy? He's head over heels about you. You have me and Keith and your other friends."

Liz turned toward me. "You know I love you, but it isn't the same. And I feel the same way about Randy as he does about me, but I will not pull him into my problems.

"He deserves not to have to look over his shoulder until this is over. And I also believe it would be the fastest way to lose him."

I patted her knee. "Let's change the subject. Tell me about your last twenty-four hours."

"The man was nice. I know it sounds weird but he treated me with respect and didn't push me or try to scare me to make his point. Of course, there was nothing nice about shoving me out of the truck on the top of a forest trail in the pitch dark."

"Tell me what he said."

"I'd rather not go over it again. I can tell you how much it unnerved me to see the exact birthmark as

Mick had and in the same place. Then he told me I didn't know anything. He said it was a family trait. He said there were five brothers and he was the last one alive."

I slowed down and glanced over at her. "You were that sure he would let you go?"

She laughed. "He didn't strike me as a total psychopath. I asked him his name and all he would give me was, Justin. And he said for a second time, Mick didn't do anything wrong. He had the unfortunate luck to cross paths with a group of people who didn't care about families; only money.

"He said Mick made a grave and fatal mistake when he was searching through the house he grew up in and found something that would unravel the entire scheme. I ask him why he didn't just come right out and tell me the story and he said, *because I like life, find what I hid. When you do, no one will have to tell you what it is. Take them immediately to the FBI. It names names; they need to be stopped before they know you turned them in.*

I didn't know if I should tell her Justin was dead or not. Maybe I should let Keith or Randy tell her.

"Two men dead, one of them a man I knew for twenty-seven years but didn't know at all."

She already knew about his murder.

"The rest of the night, after he left me in the cold with no food or water or a coat, I tried to break into several cabins I came across, to no avail.

"I decided I could stay on the trail I found and so long as I kept moving downward I would eventually run into someone. Problem is, it began to rain. I slipped on the gravel, slid off the trail and hit my head on a rock. You know the rest."

Nutmeg, who had been asleep on the back seat the last few hours began to whine and whimper. I pulled off the road, she bounded out of the car. Within minutes she came back and went to sleep.

This time she didn't want to be in the back alone and climbed over Liz, laid down between us with her head on Liz's lap.

I helped Liz get settled in her apartment. When she skidded on the gravel on the mountain path, she caused the worst, biggest, bruised raspberries, one on each leg. The bump on the head she acquired when she hit the unmovable bolder swelled more as we talked about it.

I fixed her a soft drink, some chicken noodle soup, an icepack, and laid her phone within reach 1 left the door unlocked so Randy and Keith could drop in.

CHAPTER TWENTY-ONE

The sunlight streamed into my room through the open curtain on the bedroom window and woke me up. Sweat stuck my hair to my face and grabbed my cheeks and chin. Nutmeg moved off the bed and onto the floor where the sun couldn't reach her.

My dreams eluded me. I knew the nighttime stories included Liz, Mick, and Mother. I was more tired now at ten a.m. than I was when I went to bed in the wee hours of the morning.

There were three calls on my phone; Keith, Aunt Sandy and Mother. None of them left a message so I chose to ignore them and take a shower. I let the hot water run down my body until it began to cool. It renewed me.

It was nearly eleven o'clock. I'd missed breakfast and well on my way to being late for the lunch crowd.

I remembered Mother. Sandra would take care of lunch if I didn't make it down. I laid on my bed to call Keith. He answered on the first ring. "Hello sleepyhead," he said in a chipper voice. "I thought we could have breakfast. You were nowhere to be found."

"I went to sleep and other than some weird dreams I can't remember, I slept like a rock."

"There was a fingerprint on the phone that was not Liz's. We traced it to a guy named Amos Wheeler, age 68, white, brown hair, five feet ten inches and two hundred pounds. The ID said his residence was Foster, Indiana. He had to be the other man you heard in the cabin. Most likely the man who killed Justin, whose last name is Dudley.

Chad Baker, the coroner, said Justin was a DNA match to Mick. Most likely a brother. Another dead end. I have no idea why he was here, but of the people we know were involved I say Amos Wheeler killed both Mick and Justin Dudley. Is this all coming together for you?"

I didn't say anything so Keith went on. "I'd say this Amos Wheeler, and the woman in the Impala, not yet identified, steal money from trust funds, stocks, or bank accounts.

"We are waiting for the Indiana police to get back to us with the name of the owner of the Chevy. My buddy up there is busy and I'm not ready to put it out nationwide yet."

Keith took a deep breath. "After the big city, I thought I would be bored in this little town. The fact that people come in from all over the country makes it a good place to hide. I'll catch up with you later."

Next, I called Mother. "Hi Mom, how's it going?

"If you really cared," she said sarcastically, "you would have called the police or gotten me an attorney and tried to fix this mess. I'm sitting up here with no friends, and nothing to do. You and my sister don't care."

"Sure, we do, Mom. Liz Austin has been kidnapped. Mick Dudley murdered, and business is booming. I'll do what I can as fast as I can, Keith is busy trying to find the killer. Liz came home yesterday, unhurt. And don't say you are as important as Liz, because I know it and I agree, but she's been in eminent danger and you are not."

"Why would anyone take Liz? I never did like Mick Dudley. I'd better not say that in public. Next, they will think I'm a murderer. We'll talk later, dear."

"I'd like to come up and talk to you about the Dudley family. Do you have time later?"

"I don't know, Arizona. Let me check my calendar. You know I have time. Even the Price Is Right wasn't fun today."

I didn't call Aunt Sandy. I lay on my bed with both arms behind my neck and my elbows in the air. I wondered how Liz was feeling. She'd had plenty of time to go over the entire ordeal in her mind.

There were some universal reasons folks murder one another; money, jealousy, greed, and fear encompassed most of them. Most people were murdered by someone they knew. We knew the motive to kill Mick was money, and perhaps family. Now it looked more like someone was stealing money from families and keeping it for themselves.

They called these *white-collar crimes*. When murder is involved, I don't see how they could call it *white* anything.

Once this mystery was solved, I intended to get some answers about my life before I came to Moonstone Lake. It hadn't seemed urgent before.

The restaurant had few people in it when I arrived. Aunt Sandra sat at the first table with her lunch in front of her. Sara had control of the checkout register.

I went over and sat in the chair across from my aunt. As usual she had a book in her hand. She looked up. "Hi, you look better than last time I saw you. Here's next month's book club selection. Thank goodness three new women joined and you weren't missed last month. Well you were missed but, oh never mind. How's Liz?"

"Liz is fine. She is resting in her apartment. According to her, the man who took her dressed nice and treated her politely. Other than leaving her on the top of a mountain trail without protection or a jacket, that is. Now he's dead. I'll tell you all about it later. Liz should write a book."

Sandy marked her place in the book she was reading with a bookmark decorated with kittens. "How are the plans for Emma's birthday coming?" she asked.

"Louis said the only difference is he has to make more food every year. I need to quickly settle Mother's lawsuit or her friends won't be there."

Before I moved on, I ordered a cheeseburger, tater tots, and a Coke. We ate in a calm silence. I didn't want to talk about Mom. Apparently neither did Aunt Sandy because she didn't take the conversation further. I got up to leave and she slipped the book across the table to me. "I finished this, you will be missing out on a great story if you don't take it"

I picked it up and tucked it under my arm. "Heaven forbid." I said with a wry smile.

Louis had his hands in a bowl of flour. "What are you baking? I asked.

He walked over and held his arms away from his sides to avoid sharing the flour he had on his hands. "Take a guess. I believe I only have twelve baking days before Emma's birthday party. If I make five dozen cupcakes a day, we'll make it. The icing is no problem. I can make it in one batch and ask two of the line cooks to help ice them. As a matter of fact, everyone on the floor has offered to help. I think everyone wants to lick the bowl."

I glanced up at him. "Thanks. I know it is late notice, but can you make something special for me to take to Liz? She is hesitant about going out and her body is a big bruised mess."

"Sure, I can. Let me think a minute."

We walked to the front kitchen counter and sat on stools facing one another. "Would skewers of glazed honey garlic shrimp fit in?"

"My goodness sounds delicious."

"Okay, Ary, I'll have them in the warmer by six-thirty. I'll make a few extra for your men friends too."

No one had to tell me the color of my face. It started at my feet and rose until even my ears were warm.

We elbow bumped. "Thanks Louis, you rock."

CHAPTER TWENTY-TWO

As a people watcher I noticed the same diners came to the café on the same evening every week. There was the steak crowd, the cashew chicken crowd, the ham and beans crowd and so on. Four men who I'd never seen before came, in around seven.

I don't always know every person who comes through the door, but these men were different. They all wore black pants, shirts, and dark brown leather vests with the words *My Way or The Highway* professionally embroidered on the backs.

On the front of the vests were patches with names. I'm sure they were nicknames. I doubt Brick, Chains, Rooster, and Tank would be a mother's choice for her baby boy. A chill went through me. We don't discriminate yet every bell, whistle and alarm in my body sounded.

The table happened to be in Jamie's section. I didn't want her to deal with them. I walked back to the wait station and told her to take a break, picked up her pad and headed to their table.

"Hi gentleman, what can I get for you? Our special for tonight is general or orange chicken, rice, crab Rangoon, and an egg roll. You have a choice of egg drop soup or one trip to the salad bar."

Chains looked me up and down. I knew he would never forget what I looked like. "We'll take four specials with the soup and four Cokes."

The other three looked at me but I wasn't sure they were allowed to speak.

I sent Benny over with the food. Later when I refilled their drinks, Chain said, "Thanks, sweetie."

I turned away and stood a few seconds. I knew my face was flushed but I turned back to the table and said, "My name is Arizona."

"Well, Arizona, I have a question for you. Do you know Elizabeth Austin?"

I put one hand on the table to keep my balance and prayed they didn't notice my hands shook.

"I know her. What do you want with her?"

Tank, who sat closer to me than the others put his hand on top of mine. I pulled it out from under his and looked him straight in the eye with my meanest stare. "Are we going to have a problem here gentlemen?"

They looked at one another and laughed, a little too animated.

I didn't blink or move my gaze. As quickly as they got rowdy, they became serious again. "I'm sorry, Miss Arizona. We know Miss Austin's hubby. We met when we was kids." He stopped talking and looked around. Rooster piped up and said, "Camp, we met at camp He talked about her all the time and we wanted to meet her."

At one time I would have believed him but by now we all knew Mick didn't serve time. I ran with it. "I have two questions, first, are you gentlemen from Indiana? And did you really meet Mick at camp when you were kids, because he wasn't married back then?"

Heads snapped in every direction as they tried to look at one another. As they moved, I noticed Rooster had a weapon. I felt faint.

"What makes you think we're from Indiana?"

"Because Mick spent some time there recently. I thought maybe that is where you met him."

"Oh, no honey. We have known Mick since we was kids."

I put both palms on their table and leaned down so my eyes were close to Roosters. "So, I guess you know he's dead."

It was Chains again. "We heard that and wanted to pay our respects."

"Liz is out of town, but if you want to leave your names, I will tell her you were here."

Earlier I had given Aunt Sandy the signal to call 911. When I looked up, Amanda and Randy stood by the front door. Tank saw them and whispered to the man next to him. "Could we get the check please? We have a long ride tonight."

Randy strolled over. "Are those your bikes outside?"

"Yeah, so what?" Chains answered.

I left and walked to the front. "Aunt Sandy, see if you can take pictures of those men before they leave."

She nodded okay.

Amanda stood between the bikers, Randy and the door.

"No reason to get nasty." Randy said. "I admired them on my way in. I couldn't help but notice the plates on each of them are expired. Can I see some ID?"

All four men climbed out of the booth. They towered over Randy. Any one of them could have put his arm out and Randy could have walked under it."

One at a time they each put money on the table as they opened their wallets. I didn't know whether I should have been afraid or laughed. All of them had wallets held on their belts with silver chains.

As they got out of the booth, they surrounded Randy. How I wished Keith wasn't asleep upstairs.

No sooner than I thought it, he stepped into the restaurant through the back and stood behind two of the men. Amanda came forward and said, "This is our police chief Keith...."

Before anyone could say another word, a fight broke out. The biggest guy, Tank, pushed Keith so hard and so unexpectedly he went backward over a chair and the table behind him taking three meals and three diners with him.

Randy drew his gun, as did Amanda. Two minutes later three Highway Patrolmen came through the door and it was over as quickly as it started.

The men went to jail, and the motorcycles went to the impound. Our crew cleaned the area. I moved the customers and gave them free meals and Keith headed home to shower.

CHAPTER TWENTY-THREE

"There you are." Louis said as I walked in. "I've got a surprise for you." He went to the warming oven and pulled out a casserole. "I made this for you and your friends. The couple who is getting married in the fall wanted something different, with chicken, I decided to use you as a guinea pig."

I leaned down and took a big whiff of the creation. "What is it? I smell chicken, dressing and spices. I'm ready, in this instance, Guinea pig fits me just fine. I'd better get up front and meet my guests."

All three of them were dressed in jeans, tees, and tennis shoes. They milled around and talked to Aunt Sandy.

"Anyone hungry?" I asked as I walked close to them.

They all answered yes and we headed back to my

special booth. All four of us were in good moods in spite of our evening chore ahead.

Before I had a chance to tell them we didn't have to order, Benny came by and put the casserole dish on the table. He returned a minute later with a basket of warm sourdough bread and honey butter.

"Louis is trying this out on us because he wants to serve it to some private guests."

I took the serving spoon and dished it out. They were quiet until Keith said. "Any time he wants me as a guinea pig, I'm ready. This is delicious."

Liz asked between bites. "Did you find the key to the storage unit? I decided to go to the bank and look in the safe deposit box. There is a deed to some land on the other side of the lake. I'll have to go to the County Clerk to find out what it is. There are US Treasury Bonds in my name. There must be a hundred of them."

Randy asked for a piece of bread. "You're a wealthy woman, and didn't know it."

Banter went back and forth through dinner. I sat back and watched them. I was grateful to have them in my life.

I signed the dinner ticket and we headed toward the basement.

It's not your standard basement. Its ceilings are twelve feet tall. When the lights were on the room lit up like noon on a sunny day, and lastly, it was clean. The storage spaces were made with 2 by 6 pine framing boards, chicken wire. Over the fencing clear plastic kept anyone from reaching in to pilfer. To remove anything, you didn't own, would take some planning.

Each space had a door with a padlock. Numbers were put near the top right side of each space in neatly painted numbers.

Keith made a complete circle looking at everything in his path.

"My goodness, Ari, who's idea was this?"

"My grandmother, mom's mom, as soon as she saw the basement, Mom said she had an idea. At first, she wanted to turn it into a flea market. Once she realized how much work it would be, she came up with storage units. There are hundreds of them".

If you looked down at the floor you were led to each block of storage units by more red numbers stenciled on the floors.]

Liz's family had one of the biggest units near the back of the north east corner. and on the left, a big sign on the front of it;2020.

Randy took Liz's hand. Keith and I smiled at one another. She stopped in front of a bin. It must have been 20 feet by 20 feet and reached within a foot of the ceiling. The space was packed with what appeared to be professionally wrapped and labeled boxes.

I could almost hear the group exhale. No one said a word. Liz unlocked the door. Space was limited. Randy and Liz went in, Keith and I stood on the outside. "This might not take as long as we thought," Keith said, "every box is sealed with an inventory sheet taped on the outside. I think we should move them aside one at a time and look for ones that have been tampered with. No one could open one and put it back exactly the way it was."

"I don't think so," Liz added. "For instance, here

is a box marked *Ben's pipes*. I see no reason to open it. And here's one *Homer Laughlin China,* and still another, *Wallace Flatware.*"

Randy walked up behind Liz. "The main problem, as I see it, is where do we put the boxes we have eliminated from those we haven't. There is no room in here for them. It will be a mammoth job to move them to the hall and put them back when we are done every day and haul them back out the next day. I get tired thinking about it."

I looked around. "Let me take a quick check and see what's empty. I'll have Aunt Sandy mark it rented and we will use it for overflow until we are done. Then we can move Liz's boxes back here when we're done. Once we get twenty are thirty boxes out of here, we can maneuver inside this space."

The other three thought it a good idea. I stepped away to call Sandy. She gave me a space three rows over. I told her I would send Nutmeg for the key.

When I called Nutmeg to me, Randy, Liz and Keith got so quiet I could hear them breathe. I knelt down so my head was at the same level as Nutmeg's. "Nutmeg. Go to Sandy. Come back with a package. Can you do that?"

The dog barked one time and wagged her tail. I'd guess she was bored and glad to have something to do.

I hugged her hairy neck and whispered *I love you* in her ear. "Okay, find Sandy, Now."

She left and when I looked up, they were all staring at me.

Keith said. "You have not had the dog long enough to teach her so much. Was she trained when you found her?"

"I didn't find her. I knew something or someone was behind me one morning after my jog. She trotted behind me; dirty, smelly, matted, skinny and with sores on her feet. She wouldn't leave. She couldn't have been over six months old.

"Louis made her fresh food with rice, hamburger, or chicken, sweet potatoes and apples. I can't really remember what all he adds. He still makes her food and bakes all of her treats.

"I took her to the groomer; had her spade and she hasn't left my side since. I don't have to ask her to protect me. It seems to be her life's work." Before I had time to tell them more, Nutmeg walked up and dropped an envelope on my lap.

I told her *thanks*. She laid down where she could see all of us, and I noticed where she napped, no one but the four of us could pass unless they went past her.

I am truly blessed.

Chapter Twenty-Four

Tuesday morning Liz had an interview with a famous author who rented a home on the lake for the summer. Randy had the day shift and I needed to make sure Mom's birthday went off without a hitch.

I arrived in the basement after five. Keith looked like he'd taken a shower in his clothes. "Hi," he shouted in greeting as he saw me come around the corner. "I thought no one was coming. You don't have a fan around, do you?"

"Not that I know of." I handed him an ice tea. "Louis told me you were here so I thought you might like this. Are you hungry?"

He looked down. "No, I'm too dirty to eat. I didn't find anything today. I'm getting discouraged. We are running out of time. The *old needle in a haystack* feeling."

Keith perched on a box. I sat on one facing him. "It's all I think about, day and night. It is too big of an area to narrow down."

He took a drink of his tea. "I know. Is it money, a book, a bond, stocks, a key, a combination? And if this happened after Liz's parents were killed and this place is filled with their belongings. Why would he put it in here?

"I found a note from a man named Jonathan Cole Massey, age 34, graduated MIT, computer whiz who lives in Joplin, Missouri. He is a collector of classic cars, coins and baseball cards. He once paid four-hundred thousand dollars for a Willy Mayes Topps Baseball Card.

"He has a car worth three quarters of a million and a silver dollar worth twenty-eight thousand dollars."

"How do you know all of that?"

"I'm the police. We know everything" he said. "Actually, I went to school with Mike Granger, an FBI agent out of Kansas City. He ran this Massey's name and all this stuff came up. What flagged him in the first place is that he has all of these items and no visible means of support. I don't know if he has anything to do with this or not. He appraised some jewelry for one of the people involved. He was careful enough to not sign anything or put the name he appraised for.

"To the FBI it means, murder, extortion, drugs, gambling or something along those lines is where he gets his money. He has no bank accounts, savings accounts, stocks, bonds or background.

"It is like he showed up one day, fully grown with a social security card, a car, a big house and no background. There is an appraisal from him for a ship's table in one of the boxes also; labeled, hobbies."

I stood. "You know that changes everything, right?"

"How do you mean?"

"Any of those three items could be stashed anywhere. It takes little space to hide a coin, a car title or a baseball card."

Keith stood, walked over to me and moved into what I considered my space. I took a step back. "Seems everyone Jonathan Massey comes in contact with dies. My friend says his father was James Massey of Massey Steel. Mr. and Mrs. Massey were killed in a house fire when Johnny boy was nine. There is no record of them ever having a child."

"His first wife was Dana Lloyd."

I put my hands up to my mouth. "The designer's daughter who was shot for no apparent reason as she left one of her father's shows?"

"One in the same," he answered. "I don't know if you remember But Marshall Lloyd killed himself three days later and Jonathan ended up with everything. So, I'm thinking with a steel company that is out of business and no one can check. And a dead wife whose father left Jonathan a fortune, he doesn't need money.

"He sold her dad's designs for over fifty million dollars. With his wife and her father's deaths I'd say he could probably have anything he wanted without killing anyone."

"I agree with you but some people never have enough. Or Jonathan is mad because Mick put one over on him. And who is Sammy DeLuca?"

Keith raised his eyes to look at me but left his chin down where he held a piece of paper from one of the boxes in front of him. "I think they are one in the same. I think it's why no one claims to know what he looks like. I don't know what kind of game they are playing but I wish I didn't have to play with them."

Liz and Randy showed up an hour later with a tray of sandwiches and Cokes Louis had ready for them as they came through the kitchen.

We all picked a box as a table and had a picnic in the storage unit. Keith told Liz about the new developments earlier in the day and of course Randy was read in.

"Liz says Jonathan Massey isn't the one who kidnapped her so now there is another person involved." Keith held a picture in front of me and I recognized him immediately. It was a picture of Chains from the motorcycle riders the day before. "Have you seen this man before?"

I glanced toward Randy. "Don't you recognize him?"

"No," he answered, I don't think I do." He took another look at the picture.

"Cut his hair, remove the beard, and take the gold off of his tooth and you have Chains from the motorcycle riders."

Randy took the photo out of Keith's hand and looked at it again. He didn't say anything for a long minute. His face turned a pretty shade of scarlet. "Some cop I am. I didn't pick up on it at all. You are right though. It is him. I wonder what the idea of coming to the café was."

"Intimidation would be my guess. I wonder what Mick's killing is really about? Here's what I think. We need to learn everything we can from Mick's past. This goes much deeper than money"

Liz sat quietly and munched on her bacon-cheese burger and watched the goings on. "Why intimidate me? I don't know these people and I haven't seen Mick in five years, not so much as a letter or a phone call. I saw to it through the courts." Liz's voice rose in pitch the more she spoke. "Let me see the picture." She leaned toward Keith and he handed it to her. She put down her sandwich and moved her hand over her mouth. "The man in the picture is the one who took me out of town and then up to the mountain."

Keith picked up a manila envelope, reached in and pulled out another picture. The one Liz had helped the police artist sketch. He handed it to her. "Do you think these are the same two men or not?"

Liz took a picture in each hand and looked back and forth between them several times. Tears filled her eyes and spilled down her cheeks. "Do you think I'm part of this?"

Randy moved over to sit next to her. "Keith only wants to find out what you have to do with this murder." Before she could speak again, he said, "I don't think you know anything about it. If you do it is a hidden memory and we need to dig it out. You don't happen to keep a journal, do you?"

"Yes, I do. I'm a writer. I've kept a notebook every year of my life since I was old enough to write. Let me ask a question. You are saying a man took me to a cabin in the woods, left me alone, which he did, came back disguised as another man to talk to me.

When he had me thoroughly scared and pledged to help him find his property, he made the elaborate change back to his first disguise and took me to the mountain top."

"That's what I'm telling you. The thing is we don't know why. If we had more time, we could find out who Jonathan really is. Find out if his real name is Samuel DeLuca and what is his connection to Mick Dudley. We have twenty-six days."

Liz stood. "Well you are wrong. If Justin and Johnathan were the same person how did he come into the café? Justin is dead; therefore, Johnathan would be dead also."

Keith looked at her. "I guess my premise is wrong. I'm not sure why I didn't pick up on such a simple thing."

We all looked at one another. I said, "When did Mick change toward you? I know you would not have married him if he treated you badly when you dated."

"At the beginning of the third year of our marriage, he began to change. He lost his job. They said he stole from the company. He said he didn't. He said someone wanted to set him up. I didn't know what to think. He loved that job.

"He said he was going to prove he didn't do anything wrong. He came on late one night. Actually, he didn't come in until dawn. After that time, he got moody and violent. He took his anger out on me.

"When they came to arrest him, they sent the sheriff's office. Later I found out Chief Chase didn't want to be the one to do it.

"After the trial and they proved he stole cars and

sold them to a theft ring in Joplin, I went through everything he had.

"Money, lots of money. He stashed it in the closet, under the clothes in the dresser drawers, his tool box and his car. If you can think of a spot, he had money hidden there."

Keith moved closer to her. "Liz, no one thinks you did anything wrong." His face clouded and he turned away before he turned back and said, "anyone can marry the wrong person." Keith pulled himself out of whatever memory he'd been lost in and asked Liz, "Where's the money now?"

"I turned it over to the FBI. It became a federal case. They said Mick sold cars outside of the state. He swears he didn't steal from the car dealer and he didn't steal cars."

Randy smiled at Liz and in an almost whisper he asked. "What kind of evidence did they have against Mick?"

"I didn't go to the trial. I was too humiliated. Eddie Crum from the car dealer told everyone who would listen that Mick got fired for stealing.

"I could feel the eyes of the entire town on me when I walked down the street. Interviews I would ordinarily do for the paper ended up on other people's desks. I contemplated moving away.

"Long story short, Mick was sentenced to five years. The next time I saw Mick was the night at Charlie' and later as he died on the sidewalk outside my apartment."

Keith looked toward Randy. "Randy, have the State Police run a background on Stanley Cleaver. I'd like to talk to him.

"Have whoever is in the office call Eddie Crum and ask him to come by tomorrow between eight and nine."

I looked around the room. We'd gone through about a tenth of the boxes. "We need a plan. Do we finish our search here? Do we go through Liz's memories? Or do we research Mick since high school?"

"All of the above," Keith said and then looked toward Liz. "I know you don't want any of us to read your deepest thoughts and feelings. My idea is that you start the day you began to date Mick. Go through each page and write down anything you think might be important. Note any new friends, new hobbies, and the things that set him off.

"Ari, any free time you have I would love it if you would keep searching down here. Randy will help you and so will I. We will set the things we find aside and hope we find a pattern to lead us to a solution to this mystery."

The four of us spent the rest of the evening moving boxes, but didn't find anything to help with our dilemma.

CHAPTER TWENTY-FIVE

I had to do paperwork once a week and tomorrow was the day. Legally, the police, couldn't go in to the storage without the owner of the building and the owner of the belongings they wanted to search.

We would meet at Moonstone Café and Sunday Brunch, eat dinner and go exploring. Mom didn't want to go but gave her permission. Aunt Sandy needed to be at the podium on Saturday night.

I loved the times I went down to the restaurant and laughter greeted me. It was Mom and her friends making plans for her birthday party which would take place the next Sunday. If they'd had a problem last week, no one would know it. They might have been senior citizens, but they had the resilience of children on a playground.

I walked toward the back. They had the overflow

door to the private room we rented out for weddings and family reunions open. Some of the larger groups in town like The Rotary, Kiwanis, Lion's Club and The Optimists had monthly reservations. Thank goodness Sandy took care of the scheduling for all of them. Louis and I did the detail work on wedding showers, baby showers, wedding party dinners, and all the weddings.

I kissed my mother's cheek. "Glad you're having fun. Do you have your theme and colors picked out?"

"Yes. We thought *81 is the new 60.* The balloons will be pink and purple. Sandy said to make a list and she will go to the store and get what we need. I thought maybe pink and purple daisies on each table."

I made a mental note to call Bud and Bloom Flower Shop and make sure she had enough daisies.

She went on so fast she could have been talking in shorthand. "My table will be in the middle of the floor as it always is and of course the food is free." She laughed. "If you like chili-dogs and chips you are all set. And everyone loves hot dogs and chili-dogs. This gives them the perfect occasion to eat them without guilt. Did you have time to put the notice in the paper? Did you run it three days like always?"

I added the Moonstone Reflection to my note.

I scanned the group. Some of them had been around my entire life. "I have it all under control. Louis is on top of the food. We will grill the hotdogs and warm the buns outside as usual."

CHAPTER TWENTY-SIX

The rest of the week turned hectic. Mom wanted to have her hair done for her party and no one had time to take her. Sandra had to check in the grocery order. Louis had a cook who needed help with his lumpy gravy. I thought it would be out of line to have one of the servers take her. It wasn't like they could say *no*. By elimination, I got the job.

I asked her to make an early appointment so I could get back to the restaurant for the supper hour. My first mistake; she couldn't go early because she never missed The Price is Right and it didn't air until nine-thirty and if at all possible, she wanted to be back by five to see Jeopardy.

She swore if she didn't see those programs she would have nothing to talk about with her friends at lunch.

When I went to her apartment a little after ten. There were at least thirty scarfs of various styles, lengths, colors and textures on top of every surface. "Mom, what's all this?"

"Oh, Ary, I want my hair the color of my new scarf and I can't find it."

I wanted to say, you can't find your hair or the scarf, but I've learned when my humor isn't often funny to mom. "Why don't you sit down and I'll take over. Let's do this systematically. What color is the scarf?"

"Purple."

"When did you buy it?"

"Yesterday."

"Who did you go shopping with?"

"Dee."

"Did she drive?"

'Yes, but I have seen the scarf since I've been home."

"So, you tried the scarf on once you got here?"

"Yes."

I walked into her bathroom and found the scarf draped over a towel rack.

In the last two years Mom's hair had been Ocean Resort aqua, Lucille Ball red, Billie Elish green and I guess now she wanted to try Barney the Dinosaur purple. So, your hair will be purple for your party.

"Yes, in honor of the book, *When I'm Old I Shall Wear Purple*. But I'm not going with this purple. She shook the silk. I have a shade in mind that will highlight the scarf."

"I can't wait." I said.

While I waited for Mom to finish at the beauty

shop, I strolled over to the Discount Grocery and scouted around for snacks. I didn't cook. When I ate, I dropped by the kitchen and someone fixed me a plate, or I dished up my own. Sometimes I ate the special.

What we didn't have at the café was good old-fashioned junk food, Twinkies, Hostess cupcakes and those little donuts with chocolate icing the consistency of plastic. They were my favorite. I also picked up Orange Crush and Nehi grape soda. I've seen my friends pass up a beer for a Nehi grape.

Mom came out of the salon. All I can say is if anyone could pull off that hair style and color, Mom could. If anyone else took the fashion steps Mom did, they would look silly.

I have to say, she always lived life to the fullest. Rolls had reversed. I had a teenage daughter and she had a grown up to look out for her.

Once I had Mother settled down in front of her TV, Nutmeg and I went for a jog.

Our schedule had us out to jog at odd hours and my body didn't like it. Always before, I ran at dawn and dusk. I needed to get back to it.

I stopped by the kitchen and checked with Lewis about the party. The crew had already decorated the place. A huge banner ran across the outside awning and in eight-inch purple letters. Happy Birthday Emma.

Another banner said *When I'm old I shall wear purple.*

After my shower, I sat in my living room with a glass of wine. It seemed I was always on the move. Ordinarily I'd go over to Aunt Sandy's. This night I wanted to do nothing more than to sit on my couch, pet my dog, have a glass of wine and go to bed early.

Nutmeg, the world's greatest dog jumped on the couch and laid beside me with her head on my lap. Were it not for Liz's dilemma, it was the best summer I'd had in years.

Before I had a chance for another thought to float through my brain a crash sounded. I heard Liz scream, then Mom screamed. I slipped on my flip-flops and headed downstairs. On my way, I dialed 911.

The door to Liz's apartment stood wide open. Mom and Liz were huddled in the hallway. Nutmeg barked a few times and ran into Liz's living room through the open doorway. "Nutmeg," I shouted. "Come back here. You might get hurt."

She came back a minute later with a smoking rag. I don't know what it had on it, but it choked all of us. Nutmeg headed down the stairs to the front door. I ran with her to unlock it.

As we went out, Keith walked up the sidewalk. "What does she have in her mouth?" he asked.

"I'm not sure. I only know it has a horrible smell and lots of smoke. Nutmeg got rid of it as soon as she could."

"I'd better get upstairs. You should consider cloning Nutmeg."

I followed Keith with my eyes and then looked back at Nutmeg. I knelt near her. "Are you okay little girl?"

She licked my face and I hugged her. "How'd you get so smart?"

Nutmeg licked me again and we went up the stairs

to see what went on in Liz's apartment.

The bookcase in her bedroom lay flat on the floor with all the books and knick-knacks under it.

"It's a good thing you had your bedroom window open." Liz stood with something tight in her hand. "Let me see what you have." Keith continued.

"I have no idea. Mick's dead, Justin is dead. If this is about money, I don't have the kind of money you kill for."

"Enough." Keith gave her a hug with one arm and retrieved the paper with his other hand."

Carefully he unfolded it. *I know you have what we want. Let's put an end to this death and destruction. Speed up this search of yours. I am running out of patience.*

Liz nearly fell onto the couch behind her. "Does that mean someone else is involved in this? Ary, Emma, I don't know what to do. I can't sleep, my mind races all the time trying to think of what Mick meant when he said the money was his. What money? People don't usually lie on their death beds."

I sat beside her. "How is it going with the journals you found the other night?"

"They're tedious. I had no idea we were so thick headed in high school. I didn't have one conversation worth remembering."

Keith knelt in front of her. "How many more are there? Just the ones from the wedding forward. Maybe we should have had you start there in the first place."

I saw Mom quietly slip out of the room. When she noticed I saw her she wiggled her fingers goodbye at me.

"Let's let this go for tonight." Keith suggested.

"But if a stranger threw the note in the window, he is here in town somewhere."

Keith stood. "Don't worry. Steve Stax needs some extra money for a baby he and his wife are about to have. The Sheriff gave his okay so Steve is out there tonight. I'll make sure he comes by every fifteen minutes. Besides, I know you two are not shy about calling me if you need anything.

"And Liz, we can quit trying to decide why they want what they want. Obviously, Mick and Justin both victims of some sort of scam. They killed Mick because he knew who they were and it was the only way to protect himself. They killed Justin for the same reason. He tried to make them think he was there to help them but they must have found out he wasn't. All we need to do is find the incriminating evidence and help set up a sting to arrest all of them."

Liz stood on her tip toes and kissed him on the cheek. He and I left at the same time and lingered in the hallway since I needed to go upstairs and he needed to go downstairs."

I walked over to the door to the staircase, put my hand on the doorknob and said, "do you really think this will turn out alright?"

"It has too," He answered and kissed me. I couldn't stop myself, I let go of the doorknob and moved my hand to the back of his neck. I kissed him back and twirled his hair with my fingers. It all came to an abrupt halt when his radio squawked. It was his wellness check.
He smiled at me and left. He reached the sidewalk and looked up to flash me his silly two finger salute.

CHAPTER TWENTY-SEVEN

Sunday came much sooner than I wanted it too. At six-thirty a.m. Aunt Sandy and I headed toward the kitchen. Louis had cupcakes on every surface. Three of the line cooks iced them and as soon as they had a tray full someone would take it into the dining room where Louis designed a pink and purple cupcake holder. The cakes spelled out EMMA on shelves three feet high. A banner made of big pink fondant letters, *eighty is the new sixty and Emma is plus one*
Happy Birthday

Benny loved to grill and talked Louis into giving him the job for the day. Our huge grill sat immediately outside the back door, which was open. An open door into a restaurant kitchen is a big no-no but we did it on Mother's birthday every year.

Aunt Sandy said the sidewalk was hot enough to

fry and egg. and the kitchen could boil water without a range it was so hot.

On the grill we could make sixty-five hot dogs at one time.

Everyone had a job on this special day. The first two hours I would plate dishes, Sandy would set up a pick-up bar and one of the servers would route guests to the correct table to get their food. We would serve the drinks ourselves to keep the chaos down.

We took turns keeping the tables bused. We changed jobs every two hours so no one got stuck with a chore they hated and have to do it all day.

Sandy picked up a small pink bowl in one hand and its twin in purple in the other. "Louis, what are the bowls for?"

"Your sister wanted baked beans. She wanted deviled eggs too, but I told her maybe next year. Do you know what she said?"

In unison Sandy and I answered. "You'll feel bad if I'm not around next year."

We all laughed.

Keith showed up dressed in a pair of old jeans and a red Moonstone Lake Café and Sunday Brunch tee shirt he must have bought off a rack near the front door. He looked good in red. His eyes were so dark I could see reflections of the things behind me in them. I thought maybe I'd be shy around him since I kissed him back for the first time the night before. I wanted to do it again.

Louis gave Keith an apron and stood him at the condiment table "Put two packages of whatever they ask for on their plate. If we don't dole them out, each person takes at least ten. I know you'll get bored, but the time will fly."

Liz wanted to bus tables. I told her I considered it the worst job in the place; after scraping dishes.

"Oh, Ary I've always wanted to work at a place like this. You said it's only two hours. I can do anything for two hours."

Randy took out the trash. I know it turned out to be harder than he thought because we used all paper products for the day.

By eleven the dining room and the overflow were standing room only. People stood outside and around the corner. I glanced at my watch. It was time for Mother's grand entrance.

As we did every year, we placed her table near the wall right in the middle so when she sat, she could see the entire room. Aunt Sandy and I decorated it ourselves. Behind her we put a gold filigree crown. We cut hearts out of colored paper and filled them with positive thoughts and taped them on the walls. We hoped people would linger and read some. All in all, it was a birthday fit for a queen. And Mother knew how to play a queen.

All that was missing was a staircase like the one in Gone with the Wind so she could daintily drag her hand down the banister.

Since her apartment took up half the first floor, she only had to walk from the hall way, to the dining room to show-off. Everyone stopped when they heard her. All you could hear was breathing. The diners stood, the cooks, and Louis came out from the kitchen. Benny left the hot dogs alone. Nutmeg, sneaked into the kitchen through the back door and laid under Keith.

Mom stopped in the entryway, held her arms straight out turned slowly so everyone could see her. She reminded me of a little girl showing off her first dress.

It took a long moment for the crowd to react. Like when you are at a recital and you can't tell if the child has finished her piece. Aunt Sandy clapped first and the entire room exploded.

Mom's hair stood straight up on top. The shade of the spiked portion could only be described as Boysenberry. The rest hung straight down held by her new scarf. I couldn't tell for sure from where I stood, I believe the scarf weaved in and out of her hair as if it was braided into it. The two shades of purple resembled a handmade woven basket.

Her pink blouse hung to her knees. A silver looped belt topped it off. Her pink and violet Pippy Longstocking leggings and pink sequined flip-flops finished out the ensemble.

Mother's not a small woman. She is short, only five feet. Her boobs could not be ignored. They preceded her into every room.

On the other hand, her smile, when she chose to flash it could light up the sky and her eyes twinkled as if they were stars.

Little by little the noise grew louder. Everyone ate and drank and it was after nine when the last person who wanted a picture with Mom had done so.

We all made it through. Louis came in and took a picture of me, Mom and Sandy, one with Mom and Louis and lastly the entire restaurant crew.

We had a picture from every year. They hung prominently in the reception area.

Aunt Sandy and I looked at them often. Not as many employees had come and gone as one would have thought.

CHAPTER TWENTY-EIGHT

My friends stayed after the party and somewhere Louis came up with a bottle of beer for each of us, himself and Aunt Sandy.

It was the first time in a long time we didn't talk about the murder. I hoped it stayed that way until the end of the evening.

Everyone wanted to help with the cleaning but Sandy and I assured them we had plenty of help who were paid to clean up. One of the line cooks brought over a tray of hot dogs, a huge bowl of chili and four smaller bowls to serve it in, He laid hands full of condiments in the center of the table.

"I know none of you had time to eat and if you don't' help us get rid of these we will have to eat them for a week."

The boys dug in. Instead of chili and a dog, they

both had chili dogs. Sandy said, "almost everyone had chili dogs." She held a small pink bowl in one hand and a purple one in the other. I have no idea what we'll do with four hundred of these bowls unless we advertise and cater some baby showers."

Randy put away two dogs in rapid succession. Keith chomped down three. Liz and Sandy and me had one. Louis joined in with us, something he never did.

"Liz, I asked, "how can you put away so much food and still weigh what? Ninety pounds."

Her face turned red. "I'll have you know I weigh one hundred and three pounds"

Randy smiled at her. "A beautiful hundred and three pounds at that."

"Isn't he sweet?" Sandy said to no one in particular.

Louis had to go. "I'm a man of habit. Sharla will wonder what happened to me. Think I'll take some of this food home to the family. It's a sure way to get forgiven."

We sat around the kitchen another half-hour when Keith's radio squawked. The table got quiet. "We'll be right there. Tell Marshall he will be in town alone awhile. Thanks Betty, we are leaving now."

Keith and Randy were on their feet. "I had a great day ladies. Sorry to end it so abruptly. But a boat and a Wave Runner collided on the other side of the lake. People are injured and one is missing. The Coast Guard requested our help."

Randy walked toward Liz and looked around. We were all right there. His face color deepened. He said, "I'll call you tomorrow. "

I knew Keith was in the car because the siren whaled.

"Have you found anything in the storage unit?" Sandy asked Liz.

So much for not talking about Mick, I thought.

"I only have five small boxes to go through. I'm over my obsession to do it all alone. If you ladies want to help me so I don't have to spend any more nights in the dungeon alone, I'd welcome you with open arms."

"Okay with me." I said, "Benny needs extra money and wants to open all week. It means I don't have to be back here until one tomorrow."

I looked toward Sandy. "And you?" I asked.

"I'm off tomorrow and I could use an adventure."

Liz and I both gave her a look. "Don't even say that. I could go my entire life without another adventure like this one."

We each went to our apartments to change and agreed to meet by the back entrance in half-an-hour. Liz was the first one back. When I walked in, she looked relieved. "I was never afraid of the dark until I found Mick's body."

I stepped up, bent down and gave her a friendly hug. "That would have scared the strongest of men."

Aunt Sandy came in and we headed outside to the basement storage.

Liz was right, there were about a dozen more smaller boxes. We each took one and sat down where we could find a seat and began to look through them.

We found nothing. Tears ran down Liz's face, "Now what? If there is nothing here, I don't know where it could be. Worse, I don't know what we are looking for."

Aunt Sandy was by her side when I stood. "Listen Liz, they aren't going to do anything to you. They don't know what it is either. It's why they threw the smoke bomb the other night."

Nutmeg barked and nuzzled Liz.

"She's right. They want to intimidate you but not scare you off. Without you they have nothing. I'm praying Keith will have more information on the players and Mick. I know this is going to turn out okay. Keith and Randy will go after them before they come after you. I just feel it."

We left Liz on the first floor and went up to our apartments. My phone rang as soon as I closed the door. It was Keith. He filled me in on the accident. Nutmeg was not too happy about it. She'd been with people all day. I let her out a couple of times during the day but she came right back.

Then she ended up in the basement with Liz and Sandy. She was not prepared to wait patiently for me to take her for a run. She whined and pawed at my foot.

"I'm glad it all turned out. No one seriously injured sounds like a miracle. I don't want to cut you short. Nutmeg wants to go for a run and it isn't getting any earlier."

Nutmeg gave a high-pitched chirp.

The other end of the phone was quiet. Keith was upset, I could tell. "You're going to run at midnight? I thought we had talked about it."

"We did. But tonight, it's a necessary. We won't be out late. I promise I'll take my phone and flashlight. I'll talk to you tomorrow. I didn't wait to see if he said anything else.

I took a breath of the clean, cool outside air. Keith didn't realize this small part of the world was my home. I could run anywhere on the Boardwalk blindfolded and still not have a problem. Besides, I had Nutmeg the wonder dog with me.

CHAPTER TWENTY-NINE

I managed to revive my jogging regimen. Within a week I was back to a six a.m. and a 10 p.m. run every day. Not only did I feel better but so did Nutmeg.

The dog didn't complain but it couldn't be fun for her to spend her nap time under the desk in front of Sandy's feet. She was a regular there now and many people called her out from her hiding place to pet her head. Small children merely ran around to Nutmeg's side and threw themselves at her. She never barked or growled at them. She wagged her tail and took it all in stride.

We'd only been back from our nightly run a minute or two. Nutmeg was in the kitchen drinking from her water bowl. I had my shoes off and trying to decide if I wanted a glass of wine or a hot bath.

I heard a low growl from the other room. Nutmeg

walked toward the front door in a stealth manner and her rumbles became louder. When she reached the door and began to sniff around, she wagged her tail and turned in circles as she did any time she felt good.

One advantage to life in a locked apartment building was no one could get in unless they identified themselves and someone released the lock to let them in. I'd given Keith my passcode when one of our chefs was involved in a homicide. So far, he'd only used it once when we were all in a hurry to get in the building and he beat everyone to the door.

After a glance at my Fitbit I narrowed it down. Sandy and I lived upstairs and Mom and Liz lived down. It was too late for Mom, Aunt Sandy met someone at the book store the week before and they were out having coffee. Keith had no reason to be there. It had to be Liz.

I unlocked the door and Nutmeg ran circles around her in greeting. The look on her face told me it wasn't a pleasure call. She had her hair braided which she often did before bed. It gave her hair waves in the morning.

She had on pajamas. The pant legs looked like a zebra. The white top had a cute zebra head painted on it with fake jewel accents. She looked like a young girl at a slumber party.

She had a death grip on something she held in her hand. "Come in. Everything okay?"

Liz hesitated at the door. "I should call Keith but it isn't important enough to wake him up but I can't keep it to myself until morning."

I pointed to the living room. "Have a seat. I was

about to get a glass of wine. Want one?"

She shook her head *yes* and disappeared toward the other room.

I poured two glasses of Moscato, my favorite, and sat one on the end table beside her. She took a long drink and sat it down before she looked up at me.

I chose the easy chair across from the couch she sat on with Nutmeg who had jumped up beside her.

"It's about Mick. I was going through my journals. I noticed the lining of the cover had been pulled apart and there were papers inside. I took them out." She handed them to me.

I read the papers then sat in my chair with my mouth open. "We know for sure Mick wasn't Mick."

Her hands shook as she reached for the papers. "It is definitely a DNA test done on Mitchell James Dudley on September 13, 1996. That would have been his eighteenth birthday.

"It says here his real name is Alexander Reed Pierce. The only child of Martin Reed Pierce, and Jessica Rose Pierce (Randel) This other paper says Martin Reed Pierce and Jessica Rose Randel were married June 15, 1980."

"It is a notarized will. It leaves forty million dollars to Mitchell James Dudley, on his thirty-fifth birthday. It was written by Mitchell, senior in the law offices of Dinwidde, Black and Foster of Indianapolis.

"How do you think his father went from homeless to a millionaire twenty-years later?

I looked at another piece of paper. "This is a DNA test on him and his mother a few days after his birth. It had to be to establish paternity."

Liz looked tired. "There are two more boxes of papers down in the basement. The Sunshine Hotel and Water Park is unveiling a new attraction at noon tomorrow and I need to be there.

"You know Ary? When this all began, I had a pang of guilt and remorse about what could have been between Mick and me. The more I get into his past the more I realize my best friend since second grade didn't trust me enough to help him."

. "Why do you think he didn't or couldn't tell me?

"Knowing what we know now, I'd say he was trying to protect you. Let's look up his dad and see what we find. It says here he was born in Gary, Indiana."

My laptop sat on a desk in my bedroom. I got it and sat it up on the kitchen table. Liz pulled a chair up next to me.

There were over two million articles under the name I entered. I added Gary, Indiana and a headline appeared.

A homeless man from Foster, Indiana had the shock of his life when a Power Ball ticket he bought at the local Piggly Wigley won the $750,000.000 jackpot. When asked what he intended to do with his windfall, he answered he intended to set some aside for his son, Mitchell James Dudley, Jr.

Liz stood and began to pace around the room. "We now know how Mick got the will. I bet he researched and found the law firm and proved his identity."

"I'm sure Keith knows all of this and more."

"I'm sure he does. We can talk to him in the morning. If it were my investigation, of course, it is not; I'd find the lady in the Impala, and the people who raised Mick. If I didn't get the answers I needed there, I would look into Justin Rust.

"We know everything but who the masterminds are, who sets up the accounts and who gets the money. The three things I'm sure got Mick killed and then Justin."

CHAPTER THIRTY

Nutmeg and I were ready for our jog the next morning but I couldn't get my mind off of Mick. My pea brain could not come up with a reason why the police staged a prison sentence, where he went for five years and why he came back.

Two hours later when I arrived at work, Keith and Liz were deeply involved in conversation. They sat in my private booth. I took it as an invitation to join them.

I went on with my chores first. There wasn't much for me to do. The reward for having one of the ten longest running family owned restaurants in the state.

Aunt Sandy handled the money for years. She went to college and became a CPA though she would not have had to since she'd been trained by her Aunt years before.

I poured myself a cup of coffee and slipped in the booth next to Keith. He looked up and smiled at me. "I wondered where you were."

"Making my rounds to assure myself everyone came in and things are running smoothly."

"I'm surprised you're up," Liz laughed. "thanks for listening to me last night."

"Liz told me about the papers she showed you. I'm going to call my buddy at the FBI and find out if he knows anything about the disappearance of Alex Pierce. Liz said you and her looked up the articles when the boys went missing. Those are just the skin of what really happened. I'll get the entire story from the FBI.

"A man claimed Mick's body yesterday. He paid the bill and left in a hearse. Best I could do at the time was take down the license plate number. The hearse is owned by Harris Funeral Home, Gary, Indiana.

"Randy called the funeral home and they said they were sorry. The service was private and they were not at liberty to give out any information.

"I'm on my way to Mick's family home, now. Do you know anything else about them except they don't speak English?"

"No. Mick never wanted to talk about them. They were not part of the wedding either. I have wondered for years if they actually exist."

Keith twirled the pencil between his fingers. "They could have been young, in their late twenties or early thirties even. I couldn't find a listing for anyone named Dudley in town. They aren't on the tax rolls, there are no social security cards or job listing for anyone by the name of Dudley."

Liz blushed. "I guess I'm not a very good investigative reporter. They were not important to Mick and so they weren't important to me. Since he's been dead, I've been too busy to give them any thought until last night when Ari and I realized his house number was the combination that unlocks the case these books were in."

Keith stood and pushed his chair under the table. "I need to go. I'm already late for report then I'll head out to Mick's house. It would be hard to live in a town for years and not interact with anyone.

"As soon as I hear from my friend .at the FBI I'll call. How long will it be before you can go through the last box in the basement?

"I'll take care of it this evening. I have a busy day at the office today."

Liz looked at her watch. "I have to be at the Sunshine Hotel at noon. They put in new water park attractions and I need pictures and quotes. You know Ary, I have run his last words through my mind a thousand times *I'm not Mitchell*. Why did he keep a secret like that from me? "

CHAPTER THIRTY-ONE

I had no idea why Mick's folks picked Moonstone Lake. I believe I would have chosen New York, San Francisco, or Atlanta, somewhere with hundreds of thousands of people so I could live in obscurity.

Moonstone Lake came into its own when a famous sports figure came to vacation at the lake and no one bothered him with autographs or interrupted his dinner. No one followed him around for autographs or stared at him while he ate.

News got around and we began to garner a big celebrity business. Pretty soon, non-famous folks began to make reservations. If the stars were talking about it, and they were; it must be a great place. We were in People three or four times a year when the paparazzi followed a big wig to the lake.

I wanted so much to abandon my post and run

upstairs to my computer. I told myself to wait until I heard from Keith. It wouldn't hurt me.

Before I could search for anything, I needed to give some attention to my job. I went in the restaurant by way of the front door and visited with Aunt Sandy. Nutmeg quickly crawled under the desk and sprawled out for a much-needed nap.

"Ary, I thought maybe you ran away. Am I going to have to nail your feet to the floor for you to stay in one place long enough to talk to me?"

I shook my head toward her. "I guess it has been a long time. How about we go to Hug-A-Mug in the morning for breakfast and catch up."

She grinned at me. "Are you buying?"

"Sure, I'll buy." She hugged me. "Okay, see you at seven. I need to run first."

Aunt Sandy looked me up and down. "How much do you weigh now? I swear, you are going to run yourself into nothingness."

"Actually, I'm up to one thirty-five."

"I'd have to see the scale for myself. I think it's more like one fifteen."

"Muscle weighs more than fat."

She reached over and squeezed my arm. "I guess you're right. There is certainly not any fat on your body." She looked at me. "I can't run, but I began to walk an hour a day with Martin. I know you haven't had time to notice, but I've lost five pounds."

I looked her over and made her turn around so I could look at her. "I see it. Sorry I didn't notice. Lot's going on. I know it's no excuse to ignore my very favorite aunt in the whole wide world. Tell me about Martin."

She reached over and gave me a hug. "I'm your *only* aunt. We're about to get busy so I'll tell you all about Martin in the morning. Now run along."

I took a few steps and stood at the entrance to the dining room. A steady flow of diners came in and out. Most ate the lunch buffet.

I put an ad in the paper every week. We would have been busy regardless but Mom taught me to pay back the town. Everyone ate at Moonstone Café. We didn't buy much in town. The bulk of our food came from one of the restaurant suppliers in Stanfield. During the farmer's market season, Louis bought as many fresh items as he could from the locals.

We bought our specialty bread from The Amazin' Glazin' Bakery and so on up and down the Boardwalk. At the front of the café we had a display of flyers from the shops with sales and coupons.

The most popular discounts were the ones we printed for each business. We spotlighted one each week, *present a receipt from The Plot Thickens Book Store and receive a free dessert* **from Moonstone Café.** Once we spotlighted everyone, we began again. It helped them but it helped us more in good will.

I loved Moonstone Lake, the café, my friends and my life except for the days I became stuck in the past and wondered who I was before I was, Arizona Summers, and where my parents were.

It had been awhile since I'd been consumed with my adoption. Mick Dudley's murder and now finding out he was given to relatives, opened up my insecurity about my identity. Emma didn't strike me as someone who would take a child illegally but why wouldn't she tell me?

By the time I closed the café, let everyone out, checked to make sure all the ranges and dishwashers were off and the dining room shined; Aunt Sandy had finished the bank deposit.

I couldn't wait to get to my computer. I wanted to find out all I could about Alexander Pierce. And look up more kidnappings in the greater Chicago area."

Aunt Sandy and I left at the same time. I left her at her apartment door, said good night. I assured her I would be at the coffee shop in the morning, promptly at seven.

Quickly I changed into running shorts, a tank top and my running shoes. Nutmeg waited, not too patiently, with her leash in her mouth. She never wore it, but there was an ordinance against dogs running loose so I always had it with me in case someone made a fuss.

After we ran, I took a quick shower, fed Nutmeg and put on a pair of blue sleepy shorts and a faded blue tee. The laptop sat on the corner of the desk in the living room. I unplugged it, carried it to the couch, propped myself on a few pillows and put it on my lap.

I sat up straighter and patted the other end of the couch. Nutmeg jumped up and laid down. I straightened out my legs and rested my feet on her back.

I switched my attention to the Dudley family. Keith had the right information on no Dudley owned property, paid taxes, applied for a driver's license or had so much as a parking ticket in Moonstone Lake; not in the entire state as a matter of fact. Dudley is not in the top five hundred surnames in the United States.

I didn't pay attention to it before but Mick kept a very low profile. In the yearbook he only appeared once; his senior picture He played golf one year in high school but was absent for the photo.

Chapter Thirty-Two

I didn't sleep well. Mick's dead body floated around in my dreams in a warehouse and steak knives flew through the air. I dodged them in my sleep.

My own ragged breath woke me up. I slipped on my running clothes and headed out the door. I hoped it would help my vivid dream fade.

I focused on what I had to do in the next hour. It was a lot but I needed to keep busy. I had to finish my run, shower, dress, feed Nutmeg and be at Huga-Muga Coffee shop on the Boardwalk before Aunt Sandy. In the twenty-five years Aunt Sandy had been my confidant, I never knew her to be so gaga over a man.

With Liz's problems, Mick's death, and Mom's brush with the law and her birthday, I had horribly neglected my aunt. Mom always said *we all have twenty-four hours a day and we manage to spend it as we want. If someone or something is important to you, the time will be available.* In her opinion my other activities would not keep me from Aunt Sandy if I really wanted to be there. I loved my mother but some of her philosophy didn't ring true for me.

I chose an outside table so Nutmeg could stay with me, ordered a Chi Latte for me and a green tea with honey for Sandy. No sooner did I set them on the table than I heard her come through the front door and greet people on her way through to our table.

I waved as she turned the corner and came outside.

"Well look at you, she said, not only are you here on time but you ordered our drinks. Want some breakfast?" She asked.

"I ordered bacon and artichoke souffles. They should be ready in a minute. While we wait tell me about Martin. Is he a Knight in shining armor?"

"Now Ary, you know I am the kind of woman who doesn't need a man to complete me. I believe it is why Martin is so appealing. He owns a beautiful home on Lakeside Drive, is a retired electrician, and an avid reader."

"Sounds like a guy right up your alley. Why did he move to Moonstone Lake?"

"He came here as a child and loved it. He and his family were here most summers as his three boys grew up. His wife became ill and died ten years ago. When he retired he found himself dreaming about living here."

She stopped when Tiffany brought our food and a treat for Nutmeg.

"How long have you two dated?"

"Geez Ary, it sounds so childish, dating."

I laughed at her. "What else would you call it? You're too young to call it courting."

We didn't have time to discuss the man further. I looked up. There stood a man who could pass for a cross between Steve McQueen and Kevin Costner. At about five feet ten, one hundred and eighty pounds he had a stealth body with a little softness that betrayed his age.

I couldn't tell how much of the wrinkles at the corners of his eyes were from his constant smile or age. He wore a white polo shirt tucked in, a thin black belt, and jeans, well-worn in all the right places.

Aunt Sandy cleared her throat and brought me out of my trance. I realized I'd been staring. "Ary this is Martin Beacon. Marty, this is my precious niece Ary."

"Hi," I managed to croak out, "please join us." Nutmeg began to wag her tail. A good sign indeed."

My phone rang. "Excuse me." I said and I left the table to talk to Keith. "Hi, what did you find out at the Dudley place?"

"I got to thinking about how I am spinning my wheels when we know Chief Chase knows why Mick went to court, why the files were sealed and why he went to Indiana instead of jail.

"If he knows all of that, I figure he knows all the rest.

"I spoke to him this morning. He has friends at his cottage in the Boston mountains. He said he can meet on the weekend. He asked about you and said I should bring you along. He also okayed Randy and

Liz. Would you like to ride along?"

"You know me. I love to be in on the discoveries. When are you driving up?"

"Tomorrow afternoon. It's about a four-hour drive but he says he has plenty of room for us to stay if Randy and I bunk together. He said we could join him for breakfast. What do you say?"

"I say give me an hour or so to work out the café schedule and I'll try my best."

I went back to the table but Sandy and Marty were deep in conversation about some author they were both enamored with.

My latte and souffle were cold and I needed to get to work. "Martin, happy to meet a man who makes my Aunt Sandy smile. I need to go to work."

"I have the lunch and dinner shift so I'll see you later." Aunt Sandy said as I turned to go.

CHAPTER THIRTY-THREE

Chief Phil Chase occupied Keith's position before him. He and I solved cases together. I considered him a dear friend.

The four of us left Moonstone Lake at noon. The Catoosa County Sheriff's office agreed to patrol for the weekend.

One of the locals told Keith of a tiny, hard to find, café on the way to the Chief's cabin. Its claim to fame was pie. Keith loved pie. Give me chocolate cake with fudge icing anytime. I acted excited because he seemed so happy, he might get a piece of gooseberry pie like his grandmother made

We rode in a compatible silence. I wanted to ask him about his old job, how he managed to end up Chief of Police in our little hamlet and why he turned sad when anyone mentioned the past. I guessed it to be a subject he would have to approach first, if he ever did.

Randy and Liz talked and giggled like a couple of kids in the back seat.

The restaurant was not a disappointment. We ordered the special, a Chicago style hot dog, tater tots, milk shakes and pie. The pies were displayed in a case along one wall. I decided on Lemon Meringue, Keith found his gooseberry, Randy took pecan and Liz chose French silk.

The scenery could take your breath away. We stopped at two overlooks. We pulled into Phil Chase's driveway about seven.

I didn't remember how much I missed talking to him until I heard his voice. He greeted me with a hug and Keith with a handshake. Randy worked with the Moonstone Police under Chase. Liz knew him also from the times she interacted with the police on crime stories.

The cabin stood three stories high. The entrance opened into a great room mostly crafted of wood. A stone fireplace sat in the center of one wall with alcoves on each side to hold firewood. Past the great room I could see the kitchen. All of the pots and pans and even the food sat on open highly polished shelves. The walls were full of paintings by Native American artists like Bill Rabbit, Oscar Howe and Woody Crumbo.

No heads of dead animals adorned the walls. The windows started at the floor and went to the ceiling. In front of each there hung an elaborate dream catcher.

Each chair had an overstuffed cushion in Native

American print as did the couch and a window seat by the front door. Above all, it made me relax.

Chief served me and Liz a glass of Moscato. "You remembered," I said.

He smiled and handed a beer to both Randy and Keith.

He sat in an overstuffed rocker with a gorgeous Pendleton throw draped on one arm. "I will guess you are here because you are stumped by the Mick Dudley case. First, I'll tell you it is his own fault they came after him. He'd been warned for years to let the authorities handle it. The case was nothing he could handle. The FBI has been investigating for twenty years and until recently, they could do no more than track the people and money involved."

Keith took a long pull on his beer. "It sure is different than anything I've ever come across."

"I'll do the best I can to tell you all I know. It's a long and complicated story so get comfortable," he said, "it's quite a ride. Some of what I am going to tell you we knew about all along, other parts we learned later. Some as late as last week.

"I don't think you will have any problem following me but if you do, feel free to ask questions. Anyone want a refill?

We all said no.

"Mick Dudley, was one of five boys born to Mitchell Dudley, Sr.

His father worked hard to keep food on the table and a roof over his family's heads.

Mitch Senior lost his job because of an industrial accident. The entire family became homeless. Mick mother died of dysentery; most likely from drinking dirty water. The situation got worse and worse for the family.

"When Mick turned six years old, his dad won a Powerball jackpot of well over one hundred and fifty million dollars. By this time, he had only two sons left; Mick and Justin." Liz put her hands to her mouth in stunned belief. "If they knew he was given to the people who raised him because his folks were homeless, I would have understood more about the way he acted."

"They gave him away to keep him safe. One of the boys was killed in a robbery, one overdosed and the third one was killed in a gang war. Life on the streets."

Chase looked Liz in the eye. "His dad wanted to protect him yet he had lost so much already, he didn't trust himself to keep them safe,

"The boy moved to Moonstone Lake when he turned seven. He gave an old Army buddy a million dollars to raise the boy and gave him some papers to give the boy when he was twenty-five.

"The man who took him in never told his wife or the boy why he was there." Her husband took the name Travis Dudley. He was a boat builder. He did his best to raise the boy. Mick didn't know he had a brother until years later."

"Travis's wife wouldn't go to school functions, join civic groups or make friends., Travis, had a fine reputation as a boat builder. There are at least ten Dudley boats on the lake today. Look for the expensive ones.

"Travis loved his wife but he was a hard man. His wife was terminally saddened by her inability to have children. Mick should have been a blessing to her. She and her sister were extremely close as children and she spent most of her time thinking about her sister who she was estranged from."

Chief Chase got out of his chair and went toward the kitchen. He filled our wine glasses, got the men another beer and said we should all stretch, it would be a long evening.

"It was a stressful childhood for the boy. When Mick turned fifteen, his dad would let him go with him to deliver boats. On this particular trip they pulled a trailer to Chicago and took time to do some sightseeing in Indianapolis, Quincy, and Rockford on their way back to the lake.

"Travis liked truck stop food. They would stop, eat, use the showers and move on. On two occasions Mick bought crime magazines, the Enquirer and The Star.

"Mick was a bright boy. As he read the stories about people losing all they had to some cyber criminals; he began to believe he was one of the misplaced children whose parents sent them to live with family because they couldn't support them or they were now homeless. He was eleven then. It took him three years and multiple trips with his dad before Travis let the boy have some afternoons off alone to explore the cites, they were in."

Keith said, "poor kid."

I stood and walked around the cabin; looked out the windows and sat back down ready to continue. Randy and Keith used the bathroom.

"Mick went to the FBI office in Chicago and told them he thought he came from one of the homeless families who had their money ripped off by a crook. They took his finger prints and a DNA sample. They told him to come back next time he was in town. They gave him a card and told him he could call and get his information in a month.

"Now we are talking about a young man who only knew one set of parents. Mick loved them.

"His torcher ended up being what he found out about his family.

Chief looked at Liz. "You most likely knew Mick better than anyone in the world. I'm sure you came up against his black and white thinking more than once. To Mick things and people were either good or bad. Since they never mentioned his family to him, he branded them bad.

"The authorities checked his DNA and came up with a match to Mitchell James Dudley of Columbus, Indiana.

"Mick insisted he see his real parents. The FBI refused saying it wasn't the right time. When in reality they didn't want to tell him over the years the family got split up and most of them were dead. Swept away in a tide of vagrants, they told him. He went back to Moonstone Lake, lived quietly, graduated from high school and married Liz. All the time he researched all he could find out about his people.

"One of the agents became friends with Mick over the years. They chatted and the man let it slip they knew where his mother was buried. He wanted to see his mom's grave. The FBI stopped him. I tell you, there was nothing going to keep that man from his mother."

"Even though it was wrong, a couple of agents went rogue and set up a fake criminal charge, convicted Mick in a hearing that never took place and relocated him to Columbus, Indiana and were going to put him with his father.

"Are you all ready to take a break? I love to sit on the porch this time of the evening and watch the wildlife. You'd be surprised at the variety of animals I see. As an extra added bonus, the biggest meteor shower of the year is tonight. I'd be remiss not to share it with you."

We all took a potty break, Phil made popcorn and we adjourned to the balcony. We were not disappointed.

The deck extended well into the trees and had several built-in areas so you could look straight down to the ground. When Chase turned the lights off, you couldn't see your hand in front of your face. The moon waxed toward full and shined behind us. We sat to watch the show. I would nominate the night for an Academy Award.

Chapter Thirty-Four

"There aren't any houses allowed within a hundred yards of the lake and no gas motors on the boats."

I stood and walked to the railing. The stunning view took my breath away. "What do you think about Moonstone Lake now?"

Without turning, I said, "I do believe you have the second most beautiful view within five hundred miles."

We all laughed.

Small talk took most of the rest of the evening. Chase showed us our rooms. They were adjacent to each other with a Jack and Jill bathroom. Keith and Randy's room had two twin beds, ours had two full. The beds had Pendleton blankets and the floors thick animal skin rugs. I could feel testosterone throughout the entire cabin.

We followed Chase upstairs and the guys went out to get our luggage.

Keith handed me my overnight bag and looked at me for guidance. "Chief, you have been more than generous with your time and your house. Unfortunately, I need to be back in Moonstone Lake by one o'clock tomorrow. The sheriff's department is covering the lake area until one."

He looked at me. "Truthfully, I need to be back by one or two myself."

Randy spoke for himself and Liz. "We are wide awake. I'd like to hear the rest of the story."

We all switched to ice water except Phil Chase who put on a pot of coffee.

"Okay will try to condense some of it. The authorities set Mick up with a room about twenty miles from his dad, who had all the money in the world and lost it to crooked investment. He went sightseeing, barhopping and played pool.

"As luck would have it, Mick ran into a young man who had the exact birthmark on his neck. The men, Mick and Justin set off to find their father.

When he got back to his adopted family, he told them about the odd man he met. Of course, they panicked and called the woman who set up the swindle.

"Enter Dr. Judy Marlin. The FBI knew there had to be someone higher up than Amos Wheeler.

"Back to Mick; he and Justin found their father in a homeless shelter. All the money was gone and the man was on his deathbed.

"Nobody is sure how he did it, but he got the

names of several of the families who had lost everything and explained to them where their money went."

"Wow," Liz said, "it's enough to make your head spin. "I loved him but even though he was different from everyone else I knew."

"Mick knew who stole the money and who they stole it from. Had he gone to the authorities instead of trying to catch the crooks himself, he would still be alive.

"He came back to Moonstone Lake found out who told them to take care of him. They were gone. No one has tracked them down. One of the men who has been with the group tracked Mick back to Moonstone Lake and killed him before he could spill the beans. They were only waiting for Mick to grow up so they could take the money from him."

I asked," so why are these people still running around loose?"

"Well, Arizona, the FBI has been tracking the criminals and the money for years. They didn't have enough hard evidence as to where they hid the money to close in on them."

"So how will you put an end to it?" Randy asked.

"That's a totally different story. I have nothing to do with it. It's after three a.m. Let's call it a night."

The four of us went to bed without much conversation. We each had our version of what happened in our minds and no one wanted to share it.

CHAPTER THIRTY-FIVE

Liz and I were as quiet in the morning as we had been the night before. We each showered, dressed and went downstairs to the kitchen. Randy and Keith were already there with mugs of coffee in front of them. They both nodded, but no one spoke.

Chief Chase stayed busy as he fried bacon, potatoes, and whipped scrambled eggs. We heard a knock. Phil wiped his hands on a towel and walked toward the door.

He came back followed by two men and a woman in their thirties. They were pleasant looking but non-descript. The two men were about six feet tall, short cropped hair, clean shaven. They were formally dressed in tailored suits, vests, black dress shoes, and white buttoned-down collar shirts. The woman wore a navy skirt, a blazer to match, black one-inch heels and a white dress blouse.

Phil offered them chairs but they remained standing. One man offered his hand. "I'm Special Agent Matthew Kirk." He pointed to his left. "This is Special Agent Maze Adams." He leaned forward to designate he was pointing to the other man. "And Special Agent Allen Spires."

Keith and Randy stood, introduced themselves and shook hands. Liz and I stayed seated and nodded to the three. Once they were done with the introduction ritual, everyone took a seat.

"I'll cut to the chase," Agent Spire said, "we are ready to apprehend the ring leaders of the theft ring that has been ruining the financial lives of so many families over the years. Because their reach is so long and so many people are involved it has taken a long time. This case is bigger than Bernie Madoff.

Agent Maze Adams looked at me. "I want to congratulate you on your bravery for sneaking up on that cabin. I would also be honored to meet the wonderful dog, Nutmeg, I keep hearing about."

Nutmeg, who was asleep behind me stood when she heard her name and walked around the table. She barked once and put her paw gently on the Agent's arm.

"She's everything I heard she was." Maze said.

"Thanks to you," Agent Kirk said, we are able to tie Dr. Judy Marlin, the owner and president of The Family Growth Fund to the others. We have one more task we need for the four of you to do and we can wrap this up."

For the next two hours the three agents went over what they wanted the four of us to do, well, actually five.

Before they left, Agent Kirk said, "You are on your own with this. We will not be able to step up until we are ready to make the arrests. Do not talk to one another about the mission. You can't so much as whisper about it to one another.

"With the new listening devices and cell phone apps, they can and will hear everything you say. This is life and death or a lifetime in prison for them. They will not hesitate to hurt you if it will help their cause.

"If everyone is sure they are prepared we will be going. Do not acknowledge us if you see us around, not so much as a nod of the head. As soon as they know you have what they want, they will act within a few hours. Good luck to all of you,"

As quickly and quietly as they came, they were gone.

CHAPTER THIRTY-SIX

The dog and I jogged over to Pawsitivily Devine to visit the groomer. I made my usual trip to Discount Grocery to see if they had any new junk food.

I couldn't buy more than I could carry and run home. I settled for two boxes of Hostess Cupcakes, a package of cream horns, and three different varieties of chips.

The dog days of summer were upon us. It caused a weird vail immediately above the surface of the lake. As a small child it unnerved me because it gave me the sense someone could walk right out of the water and onto the sidewalk.

Now I'm an adult and I would like to say it doesn't scare me anymore. It's not true. On days when the coolness of the water meets the steam of the one hundred-degree morning I ask Nutmeg to run between me and the water.

I ran my role in the sting to catch the criminals through my mind. All I had to do was be myself and it would all work out. I took a couple of deep breaths and put it out of my mind.

My cell phone rang. When Liz popped up it read *star reporter*. "Hi, you are calling pretty early."

"I know. Are you still going to help me go through the last box of papers in the basement? I also found three more journals."

"Sure, what time do you want to start?"

"Randy wants to have dinner at the new Crab Shack on the north side. I have to laugh. There's nothing authentic about fresh sea food when we are a minimum of twelve hours from the ocean. Randy swears they fly it in fresh every other day. Besides it's Johnathon Ramboll's place. Remember Johnathon? He graduated a couple of years behind us?"

"Who could forget him. He could only be described as beautiful."

Liz laughed. "I agree, handsome just didn't do it. I'm anxious to see him. Randy says he is married and is the father of five little girls. His wife is the chef."

"It sounds like fun. What time do you think you will be ready to finish your hunt?"

"How about eight-thirty. I'll meet you in the restaurant."

We hung up. I smiled to myself. If Liz and Randy were going to dinner alone, I hoped it meant they were getting closer.

The café overflowed from breakfast all the way through the dinner hour. A steady stream of people flowed in and all day we had a line out the door and around the corner.

I took a break to check in with Aunt Sandy and make sure she didn't want or need anything.

"You'd think we were giving a gift away with every meal. Do you know what's going on in town to bring in so many extras?"

She reached under the podium and handed me a flyer. FIRST ANNUAL CIGAR BOAT RACES.

I looked at Aunt Sandy, the line waiting to check out snaked all the way back into the dining room. I offered to help. "I'll take part of these. I know we rarely open the second station, but I think now is the time."

We didn't have a lull until after eight o'clock. I'd venture to say it had to be the best day we've had since I took over. I wanted to run up to my apartment and change into jeans and a sweatshirt before Liz arrived. On my way out I saw Agents Kirk and Adams. They wore shorts, flip-flops, and carried sightseeing brochures. I made it a point to move my eyes to the next people I saw. The only thing different about me was my heart beat and I knew no one could hear or feel it but me.

Liz came bopping into the restaurant exactly on time with an electric smile that lit up the room. "Are you ready to go?" she asked. "I'm hoping this is our last night down there. As a matter of fact, we could go get it and bring it up. The journals are already in my apartment."

"I'm down with that." I answered as we walked toward the kitchen to get the basement key.

Fifteen minutes later we both sat cross-legged on

Liz's living room floor and looked at the papers in the box. "Why do people keep all of this stuff? I mean who would want it? It makes me look at souvenirs differently. I need to keep in mind that once I'm gone it will be trash."

"Geez Ari, you're cheerful tonight."

"I'm cheerful, but I'm a realist."

We worked on the box until she said, "I think I have it'"

"Let me see it."

She held it up over her head and tried to see through the envelope and read the papers inside. It didn't work.

"Open it."

"I'm not sure I want to. Don't forget, whatever is in this envelope got Mick and Justin both killed. Let's try to get hold of the people who want it, hand it over and be through with this entire ordeal."

"You mean after all of this you don't want to see what it says?"

"No, it makes us vulnerable. They killed before to keep the information private. What makes us special? They aren't going to let us go any more than the others."

"How are you going to prove to them we didn't look at it?"

"Look at the envelope, Ari. Mick has it sealed. It would be obvious if someone got into it. Here is what is says on the outside. *To Whom it May Concern If you have this packet in your hands, I am dead. Give this package to the FBI. Inside is all the information they will need to put an end to Amos Wheeler and his plan to be the richest man in the world.*

I looked at Liz. Tears streamed down her face. She tossed Mick's papers onto the coffee table.

I put my hand on her shoulder. "I'm sorry Liz."

"So am I. Had he told me about all of this we might have been able to do something about the situation. I didn't know him at all."

"I know you are hurt, but if he hadn't left you out of it, you might have been lying next to him in the morgue.

CHAPTER THIRTY-SEVEN

On my jog I saw Liz put a note in a trash can outside of the Sunshine Hotel. She turned back toward her apartment at a fast clip.

After my run Nutmeg and I went down to the lake to relax by the water. Someone sat beside me. Since Nutmeg didn't bark or growl, I knew it to be a friend. It was Liz. "I thought I saw you go home."

"You did. I noticed you and Nutmeg and decided to come join you. You looked so peaceful."

"It is much different from how I feel."

She patted my shoulder. I smiled at her. Then her cell phone rang. *Bring all of the evidence to Pier 11 outside the motel.* He talked extremely loudly. I could hear his every word. "*There is a boat docked there. It's covered for winter. Stick the information under the lid of the storage in front of the boat. Leave and don't look back.*

"I'm willing to give you every paper I have. I am not sticking them anywhere. You at least owe me the courtesy to meet me."

"I'm on a tight schedule. You WILL do as I say."

"Who has the information?" Liz said in an authoritative voice. "Listen, whoever you are; I would rather see you rot in jail, so don't push me. I'll meet you at the end of Pier 5 and hurry up. Make it a half-an-hour."

"You know when I get there, I could hurt you?"

"But you won't. I copied the papers except for the last one I didn't open. I put them in a safe place. If I don't show up at work in the morning, the FBI will pick you up."

"You are pretty feisty for a pip-squeak. "

Liz hung up. Her hands shook, her hair stuck to her face from the sweat. I wanted to tell her how brave she was but I remembered what the Agents said. I gave her a hug and headed for home.

Nutmeg whined to go with her. I knelt down to her level and whispered in her ear. I don't know how much she understood but she turned toward the apartments.

I knew the plan to arrest this man once he was at the other end of the pier. I could see it from my window.

I saw Liz walk briskly toward the end of the pier. A man sat on the edge of a boat. This was the pier where most locals tied up their boats all winter. None of them had a cover on them. Most bobbed in the wind.

The man stood and walked slowly toward Liz. My

heart raced. I could only imagine how she felt. He stopped at a crowded part of the dock. It forced Liz to move closer to him. She stood much too close to the edge.

When they outstretched their arms to make the exchange; all hell broke loose. FBI agents stood up in the boats and yelled. *Stop where you are.* Two dozen heavily armed men in full battle gear ran toward him from the shore end of the dock. *Drop to your knees. Clasp your hands behind your head.*

Almost in slow motion he followed the Agent's orders. About then I saw Randy and Keith stroll down the pier. Randy pulled Liz to him and told her how brave she was. I chose that moment to take the ear piece from my ear. The two needed their privacy.

Keith looked at my window and motioned me to come down.

CHAPTER THIRTY-EIGHT

Keith began to walk up the path to meet me. "Hi," he said and cocked his head toward the FBI, impressive aren't they."

"No more impressive than Liz." I answered.

Randy and Liz caught up with us. They were hand in hand. Arm's swinging like teenagers.

Keith put his arm lightly around my shoulder. "Anyone up for a boat ride? Let's take this one." He pointed to a Sunray ski boat, vivid red on top and stark white on top. It had a canopy to keep the bright sun off in the middle of the day. It wasn't new but in great shape. "It is mine, the marina delivered it today."

We all needed a break away from the sadness of the previous few weeks.

Keith's phone rang. "He crossed his fingers and

held his hand up so we could see it. He broke into a smile. They picked up Dr. Judith Martin and she is trying to save herself. She is giving out the names of all concerned. The rats are deserting the ship."

Keith fired up the boat and we took a spin around the lake. "Well," he said, "we relaxed them"

Randy and Liz were asleep. She had her head on his shoulder and his rested on a side window. I could hardly keep my eyes open.

Nutmeg, however, stood on a back seat with her head up enjoying the wind.

There were eight to ten weeks of summer left, depending on how the September weather came in.

I looked around at my friends and Nutmeg.

What a great life.

THE END

About the Author

Susan Keene, author of the popular Kate Nash Mystery series, lives in the Ozarks and writes full time.

She loves to cook, hang out with her grandchildren, and spend time with her numerous dogs.

Susan's new series, The Arizona Summers Mysteries are true cozies. They include a restaurant, her mother, who doesn't want to let go of the business, although she retired years earlier and her Aunt and best friend Sandy.

Nutmeg helps her solve crimes and keeps her out of harm's way. The dog is able to know what is going to happen just before it does. Some have begun to call her psychic.

Each book includes recipes for some of the dishes that were used somewhere in each adventure.

Recipes

Simple caramel icing.

- 1 cup Brown Sugar
- 1/2 cup Butter, cubed
- 1/4 cup Milk
- 2 to 2 1/2 cups Powdered Sugar
  - In heavy saucepan, combine the milk, butter and brown sugar.
  - Cook and stir over a low heat until the brown sugar is dissolved.
  - Increase the heat to medium. Do not stir.
  - Cook for 3-5 minutes until either bubbles form in the center of the pan or the mixture turns amber.
  - Remove from the heat and pour the caramel mixture to a small bowl.
  - Cool to room temperature.
  - Add caramel mixture to a mixer.
  - Gradually mix in powdered sugar until combined, creamy and the correct consistency.

(If your icing is too thick, add one teaspoon of milk at a time and mix until it is how you want it)

Easy-Peasy Caramel Cake

- 1box yellow cake mix
- 1/3 cup butter or margarine, melted and cooled
- 1 cup milk
- 1teaspoon vanilla

- 3 eggs
  - Preheat oven to 350
  - Melt the butter and cool it.
  - Add it to the rest of the ingredients in cake mix
  - Bake according to the instructions for cupcakes on the box.

(I do have a recipe for a caramel cake from scratch. Since I am not Louis, I go the easy way.)

A great snack for company
Crispy Cheese Wafers
- 2 cups grated cheddar cheese
- ½ butter at room temperature
- 1 cup flour
- ½ teaspoon ground cayenne pepper
- 1 teaspoon of Worchester sauce
- ½ tsp of salt
- 1 cup crispy rice cereal
- Preheat oven to 350
  - Mix all the ingredients except rice cereal together. Stir with your hands until the dough holds together in a loose ball.
  - Gently mix in cereal
  - Shape into one-inch balls
  - Place one inch apart on a non-greased pan
  - Press them down with a fork.
  - Bake 15 minutes or until firm

(Really good served with cream cheese, or hot jelly)

OTHER PUBLICATIONS BY SUSAN KEENE

Arizona Summers Mystery
Wedding Cake Murder(Book 1)

The Kate Nash Mysteries

Finding Lizzy Smith (Book 1)
Who's Roxy Watkins? (Book 2)
The Untimely Death of Ivy Tucker (Book 3)

Stand Alone
Tattered Wings
The Twisted Mind of Cletus Compton

Children's Books
The Adventures of Diggitty the Dog (Book 1)
Diggitty the Dog Finds a Friend (Book 2)
Diggitty the Dog Saves Christmas (Book 3)

We Are Not So Different After All

CHAPTER ONE

As I opened the door to the restaurant I heard my mother's voice echo from the kitchen. She barked orders like a drill sergeant. No telling what she was up to. She never set out to raise havoc, yet catastrophe followed her around like a puppy dog.

To stop her tirade, I walked up, stood behind her, and tapped her lightly on the shoulder. She jumped forward, turned around and put her hand over her heart. "Arizona Summers, you're going to be the death of me yet."

"Mom what's going on? Why are you yelling at the kitchen staff? And in a voice, I might add, that could shatter crystal."

She said nothing but stepped aside so I could enter the belly of the café where the food was prepared. I looked around. "My goodness, James, why's all the bread dough still unbaked? We open in less than an hour."

My mother, who now stood behind me, found her tongue and answered before the chef had a chance to speak. "We were running late. I told the cooks to dispense with the bread and to use the ovens for the desserts."

James looked my way and shrugged his shoulders.

With my hands on my hips I turned to face her. To deal with my mother could be compared to tackling a blizzard without a coat and hat.

I looked at her and stifled a laugh. She wore a teal green tank covered with a long cardigan in pale yellow. From the waist down, she wore only her underwear. Due to the length of her top I doubt the staff noticed.

"Mother, there's an order in which we do things around here. You taught it to me when I was a child and you went over it enough times I repeated it in my sleep.

"We fix the main dishes, sides, salads and the bread. Once those are finished we bake the pies and cakes. People eat dessert last. We have more time to prepare those than the main courses. I know you haven't forgotten so what's up?"

Every day it became clearer why the younger generation took over the cafe when their parent reached her seventy-fifth birthday. I was the fifth generation of Summers to run Moonstone Lake's favorite dining spot.

Some days I wondered if I would survive Emma's interference. In my childhood I called her Emma to catch her attention. Like many busy moms she could block out my constant interruptions.

Sunday brunch took my full attention. I asked her if I could speak to her in the hall. Once we were face to face I said, "I know you like to be in charge but it doesn't work anymore. Please go home and get dressed if you want to mingle with the diners. I suggest you don't do it in your under pants."

She looked down, raised her sweater a little and said, "I'm dressed."

"And you look very nice; from the waist up. I believe skirt or slacks would set off your lovely outfit better than your granny panties."

She turned on her heel and lumbered out the side door. Too many years of restaurant food, mostly desserts, had taken its toll. She looked back to get in the last word. "I don't wear granny panties."

I watched until she disappeared.

Once I heard the door close I returned to the kitchen to try to salvage the day. James walked over to stand beside me. "I'm sorry Ary. I never know what to say to her."

"I know, James, it isn't your fault. I'll call the Amazin' Glazin' and see if they can spare any bread. Meanwhile put as many loaves as possible in the ovens."

The bakery offered us fifteen loaves. I walked across the Boardwalk to pick them up.

Dottie Wittmore had run the Amazin' Glazin' Bakery for as long as I could remember. The aroma of pastries and breads wafted out to the sidewalk. I smelled chocolate, peppermint and fresh rye. I smiled to myself. You'd think the smells would mingle and give off a toxic fume. Somehow they stayed separate. I lingered outside to savor the aroma.

The bakery was full. Both cash registers had lines at least six customers deep. I waved at Dottie and stood to the side, out of the way, until she had time for me.

A young couple sat at the back under an arch in an area decorated like a wedding dome. Many brides and grooms sat there over the years to design their wedding cakes.

Stacy Young and a handsome young man were seated in two of the four chairs arranged around a small heart-shaped table. He had his hand on hers and smiled every time she spoke. What caught my eye were the two women who sat with them. I knew one to be Stacy's mother, Denise. She and I frequented the same book club. The other lady looked out of place in her purple feathered hat, long black coat, brown orthopedic shoes and white gloves.

I watched the four of them. The lady in black threw a hissy-fit. I couldn't hear the conversation but her gestures and tones were unmistakable. I knew the other three and the cake designer had to have been horrified when the bakery became dead silent and the patrons all turned to stare at them.

The woman stood and in a voice the entire shop could hear yelled. "I knew this wedding would be a joke. I should have insisted the ceremony and reception be held in Boston. There's no way this man is a professional cake designer, the church only holds a hundred guests and the reception is at a diner whose claim to fame is a Sunday Brunch."

She looked down at her son. I half expected venom to spurt from her mouth. "And I don't care what your reasoning. I refuse to allow you to have a gray armadillo-shaped groom's cake with gray icing and red cream filling."

As she finished her rude comments I thought of my mother. She had become an instant angel in my mind.

I put my hand over my mouth to stifle a laugh as I visualized the armadillo cake and its gooey filling. On her way out the woman knocked into my skinny frame which caused me to hit the wall behind me. Her feathered hat sailed off her head. No one moved. She reached down picked it up slammed it down cockeyed on her head and stormed toward the door.

She didn't offer an apology. I said an aggravated "Excuse me," as she left. She turned and glared.

Dottie called me to the counter. Fifteen loaves of various varieties of bread stuck out of two huge brown paper bags. "I thought you baked your own bread. Everything all right over there?"

"Yes we lost track of time today." I nodded toward Michael, the cake designer. "What just happened?"

"The groom's mother's a witch. I'm being kind. They've been here three separate times to pick out a cake. The wedding is in less than six weeks. His mother doesn't like anything. I swear, if someone gave her a million dollars she wouldn't take it because it would be the wrong shade of green.

"I told Michael not to put up with it. We don't need business that bad. I wonder how his mother would get along with Suzie, who ices the cakes at Discount Grocery. They're the next closest thing to a bakery within thirty-miles.

"Mike said he hated to send them away. He and

Stacy became close friends when she worked here during her college breaks."

I took the bag she handed me. "Who's the groom? He's a real cutie; he obviously has the patience of a saint if he sat through that with his mother more than once."

"Stacy introduced him as Dillon Freedman. We don't have to guess where he's from; his mother has screamed it enough. Can you imagine comparing our little town of twenty-two hundred to Boston and its hundreds of thousands of people?"

I turned toward the door. "It takes all kinds. I'd better get back. We open in ten minutes. What do I owe you?"

"Oh honey, I'll bill you. You run along."

On the way back I thought about Stacy's mom. The bride's family customarily paid for most of a wedding. Mrs. Young called a few weeks earlier to schedule a time to meet and select the food for the reception. I got a chill at the thought of having to deal with the groom's mother. At least I had seen her in action and knew what to expect.

The kitchen had settled down by the time I got back. James and one of the line cooks sliced the bread I brought with me.

The waiters and waitresses were lined up for the little talk I had with the entire crew as often as I could before we opened. I likened it to the stewardess who stands in the front of the plane to explain to the passengers how to survive a crash. They were there and attentive but I knew if push came to shove we'd all go down with the ship.

They needed a reminder more than ever on brunch

day. "Everyone looks neat and clean, thank you. Remember; keep water glasses, coffee cups, soft drinks and tea glasses full.

"Remove plates from the tables in a timely manner. You don't have to put up with cursing, abuse, touching or general orneriness. Do not handle it yourself. Keep smiling and come get me. I'll take care of it. Mitch and Sara, take section 1, Stan and April 2, Mark and Benny, 3 and Jan and Patty, 4. Good luck out there."

I didn't actually view the dining room as a war zone. We rarely had any problems.

Mom and the bread situation slowed me down. I hadn't changed out of my running clothes. I yelled at my best friend and aunt who stood at the hostess podium. "Sandy, I'll be back in five minutes."

As I went home to change I thought about my Aunt Sandy and how expertly she directed traffic every Sunday. If left unattended and allowed to seat themselves, some customers acted like a herd of cows who tried to get through a narrow gate at the same time. If it were not for my mother's youngest sister, there would be a weekly stampede nearly as dangerous as the Running of the Bulls in Pamplona.

People pushed and shoved to commandeer a table as close to the buffet table as possible. To some it equated to tickets on the fifty-yard line at a professional football game. A seat near the buffet line became prime real estate on Sundays. The closer people were seated to the food the less time they stood and line in more time they had to eat.

I hated the *all you can eat* concept. Too many diners took it as a challenge. I preferred *all you care to eat.*